The
Candle
Burns Low

Iona
Carroll

ISBN: 978-1-80440-251-1

Typeset in Georgia

Image of Author: Copyright © Zoe
Meadows Photography

Cover Design and Artwork: © Fiona
Ruiz

www.ionacarroll.com

Silver Quill Publishing
www.silverquillpublishing.com

Silver Quill Publishing

THE STORY OF OISIN KELLY

CRYING THROUGH THE WIND

ISBN: 978-1-912513-80-2

This is the tale of Oisin Kelly, beginning with his mother, Annie as she struggles to come to terms with her love for two brothers in a small West of Ireland community in the 1950's.

Married to Bernard, she is attracted to his brother, the mysterious and much misunderstood Mick. Annie's strong Catholic faith engenders a deep sense of guilt, at the same time it helps her to cope.

The story moves forwards, sometimes gently, sometimes turbulently all the time combining pathos with humour. Although *Crying Through the Wind* is very much Annie's book, the stage is set for Oisin who has a quest of his own. First Published 2014.

FAMILIAR YET FAR

ISBN: 978-1-912513-80-2

Young Irishman, Oisin Kelly, bitter and disillusioned leaves Britain vowing never to return. When he arrives in the outback Australian town of Kilgoolga his life is still haunted by past events. Struggling to come to terms with his new and sometimes frightening environment, he falls under the spell of the enigmatic Eleanor Bradshaw. Deception, intrigue and misplaced loyalty are at the heart of this work of fiction as Oisin discovers that things are not always what they seem. First published 2015. 2nd Edition 2018.

HOMECOMING
ISBN: 978-1-912513-82-6

Oisin Kelly has put down roots in the outback
Queensland town of Kilgoolga. Here his life becomes
entwined with Vietnam War veteran, Harry. Past
traumatic events affect both men in similar and
sometimes surprising ways. As Oisin discovers more
and more hidden secrets, he begins to wonder where
his life is leading, and where his true home really is.
Decisions have to be made as to which force is more
powerful. Will it be the power of love over evil that will
triumph and bring him home? Published 2018.

PROLOGUE

Dear Oisin

You always were my favourite brother.

We are the black sheep of the family, aren't we?

Both of us went our separate ways. You disappeared to the other side of the earth, never to be heard of again, and as for me, I pursued a different life.

For what I have done I feel no remorse, I want you to know that. Perhaps Frankie and Declan may understand in time. Perhaps not. And I'm long past asking a merciful God to forgive me my sins.

My only wish is that you try to understand what I have done without passing judgement. Somehow, I know you will one day.

Your flawed sister,

Mary

PART ONE

RETURN

CHAPTER ONE

As he strolled towards the rough white sands to climb over the rocks, Oisin Kelly's foot slipped. It had rained during the night and the rocks lined up in higgledy-piggledy fashion were wet; the moisture on them shimmering now under the early morning sun. Oisin paused, then he quickly regained his balance, but now he walked slower, deep in thought.

He was thinking that in all things there is a beginning and an ending. And in the beginning lies an ending and in the ending, a beginning; the circle of life, the great unfathomable mystery of it all. It was a puzzle for this gentle Irishman who had often considered these matters were worthy of a lot of thought, for hadn't he the soul of a poet? That's what his Uncle Mick told him but then Mick had his own demons. Adversity in the beginning of life often leads to triumph at the ending, thought Oisin. His own life had seen many a triumph, and in equal measure, many a trial. Now his beginning held an ending for he was back on his native soil, and at his old home, An Teach Ban, situated just a few miles from the small village of Ballybeg in the west of Ireland. Farmers for generations, the Kelly family had toiled on this land; survived the hardships and the ever changing seasons. Oisin's brother, Declan lived there now with his wife, Joyce. Declan was considered the custodian of the land for all the

Kellys. Oisin's other siblings, Frankie and Mary had left An Teach Ban as soon as they could get out. But they both considered the farm their own. It was a blessing that Declan's only son, Ryan kept it all going. The father and son prospered but not in the ways that their ancestors would have ever thought possible. They owned the land and that was everything to them. Instead of devoting all their time, and energy and money, to farming, Declan and Ryan had diversified. Now holiday cabins were built on land where once pigs used to snuffle about in the mud. The vegetable patch that Oisin's Uncle Mick had tendered for so many years had grown to over an acre, and now organic vegetables were offered for sale in an old outbuilding which had been converted to a farm shop. Declan's wife, Joyce, the Englishwoman from Hastings was the entrepreneurial wizard in all this. It was she who advertised the holiday cabins and the farm shop on the internet and it was she who organised the bookings. During the leaner autumn and winter months when the summer holidaymakers drifted away, Joyce arranged retreats for writers and artists. Here, in a converted stone outbuilding, and with the help of various tutors, it was to be hoped that the creative juices would take hold of the paying guests, and with the added benefit of hot meals provided by Joyce and her helpers, this was advertised as an inspirational setting and one to guarantee results. People came from miles away because wasn't it true that Ballybeg offered a respite for weary and stressed city dwellers, and An Teach Ban with views to the sea and Slieve Geal, the conical shaped mountain just a few miles from the farm, could be climbed easily, and who would not want to admire those views whilst breathing in the fresh country air? But in Ballybeg the Kelly family were as much a part of the land here as the rocks beneath Oisin's feet, and it was no wonder that the new look An Teach Ban prospered, for after all, the Kellys were Ballybeg.

It had been a difficult evening for Oisin last night at An Teach Ban with his two brothers, Frankie and Declan, for wasn't their mother dying, lying alone in a hospital bed in Ballybeg? Any moment now, they would hear the phone ring? Would there be anyone at her bedside to say goodbye? Would she just drift away peacefully one night and their tears come later? Their dear mother, Annie had taken a turn two weeks ago. That was why Oisin had come home. He shivered in the cool of the morning for he felt the cold and he had been so long away. At An Teach Ban last night they argued and joked and all talked at once, and somehow Oisin felt he was an interloper in the family gathering, a stranger amongst his own kin.

'Oh, c'mon, Oisin,' Frankie said. 'Will ye not take a drink, man? And drink a toast to Annie.' For Frankie, the ex-priest and now a married man had changed a lot since Oisin had last seen him out in the dusty outback town of Kilgoolga where Oisin had lived for so many years, so far away from An Teach Ban and the farm. It occurred to Oisin that his brother's piety had given way to indulgence, and the whiskey was upon his lips more than ever these days.

But then Oisin, obedient to his elder brother as always, had taken the glass full of single malt brought out specially for the occasion, and drank a toast to his mother along with the rest of them, for wasn't that the easiest thing to do, in the circumstances? And he tried to joke too, as if in the drinking and the joviality, he was no longer a stranger to his family. But the feeling stayed with him and he drank just one glassful, made an excuse to leave the room early because he was tired from the long flight from Australia. But that night, lying in the bed he had slept in as a child,

he thought of his mother, her courage and her frailties, and he was proud of her resilience.

An Teach Ban was different and yet the same. He was a giant in rooms which were once huge, now the rooms felt small and cramped. Most of the walls were painted different colours, so much brighter than he remembered, but the rooms were still the same. Lying on his back and looking at the ceiling, he returned to childhood memories. He thought about his Uncle Mick's chair. His brother, Declan had never got rid of that favourite chair so now it was a relic and uncomfortable to sit upon, but still there at the kitchen door, next to the range, and the preferred chair of the large and much loved tortoiseshell cat. Seeing the chair there in the place it had always been was to Oisin a reminder, and an uncomfortable one, of Mick and his mother and their hidden love. These thoughts were still out of reach sort of things, placed at the back of his mind, and he had kept them there for so long. Being here in An Teach Ban, they all came back to him. He remembered the shame he felt when he first discovered his mother and his father's brother in bed together. Somewhere along the line, he tried to forgive his mother but he never forgot the feeling he had had then. But who was he to judge for hadn't his life held many temptations and secrets that could never be told? That thought had helped him to forgive his mother, or perhaps to understand just a little more of the complexities of human life and relationships.

His thoughts turned to Mick and he began to focus on his uncle's face and the black patch that covered his left eye. Mick always wore his eyepatch.

That image of Mick made him feel better. Oisin had never seen Mick without the eyepatch, except at the end when Mick was laid out for all the family to say goodbye. After all, he concluded, his uncle had been a most interesting man, and a troubled one at times. It was no wonder that his mother had loved him. He remembered that it was Mick who told him he would be a hero and how proud his ten-year-old self had been to hear that, but when he spoke about it to his brother, Frankie, well, Frankie taunted him and called him, 'Frog'. No one called him Frog now. Frankie wouldn't dare. But no one knew him as a hero either. Browned by years under the hot Australian sun, he was a stranger in the Ireland he once called home. With that thought he had fallen asleep to waken early to the call of an amorous blackbird outside his bedroom window and a shaft of thin light through the curtains.

The house was quiet and it was early. He knew Declan and Joyce were up. He heard voices coming from the kitchen and the clatter of plates but he knew how to leave the house without anyone knowing. So many times in his early life, he had crept out and no one had known. He dressed quickly because the damp cold air was foreign to him now. He pulled an extra woollen jumper over his head and covered his once curly black hair, almost totally grey these days, with an old tweed cap he had found hidden at the back of a drawer, and tiptoed out of the house.

It had rained most of the night. A haze hung over the world he used to know as he made his way along the track from the farmhouse towards the main road which weaved its way along the shoreline. Droplets of the soft Irish rain fell lightly onto his cheeks and into his eyes, and he wiped his hand across his face but the moisture stayed on his skin. He felt slightly irritated and didn't know why. The road and the sea were familiar because the rocks and the sea and the wide white sands of the strand do not change. People change but the land remains the same. Behind him, Slieve Geal, the conical shaped mountain that was so majestic and so loved to everyone who lived in Ballybeg, was covered in the fine mist of his childhood memories, and, seeing the mountain, he thought of his mother again. Slieve Geal had been misty the day he, Mary and his mother returned on the train from the great adventure of London when they all went off to say goodbye to their dying grandmother. He had not wanted to return to Ballybeg then, and he had cried for he was just a young lad and the big wide world frightened him, yet excited him in a magical sort of way. Maybe his mother hadn't wanted to return either? He had never thought of that before. Maybe she had been already in love with Mick then and perhaps to stay away might have been the safer option? But his mother was loyal to his father and her children. She would always do what was right.

He wondered how she would be when he saw her now, these last few days of her life, and he knew he had to summon the courage to see her because that was what she wanted, to see him again, that's what Frankie said when he made the frantic call. Oisin and his mother had never been particularly close but the bond of the love of a mother and child was there between them, would always be here. He decided that she really did love him, despite everything, because Frankie had called to beg him to come home and that wasn't like Frankie, to beg. There was sorrow in Frankie's voice, and Oisin decided then and there that he had to make the long journey from Kilgoolga to Ballybeg.

Years ago he loved to ride his faithful pony, Bess, along the strand, and how on that last day with Bess, he had been so sad. His destiny was to leave Ballybeg and his childhood home, he knew that now, had known then. If he had stayed, he would have remained a prisoner to his environment and deep down he hadn't wanted that. Not then, not now. He was a totally different person now, perhaps wiser, and one of the reasons this had happened was that he had gone away. Life does this to you, he thought. People change. He hoped that his mother would be able to understand, and not think he was still the awkward eighteen years old of that memory. And his thoughts turned once again to the beginning and the end, and all things in between.

The sea had washed a thin line of seaweed onto the sand and the gulls were busy, pecking away. When they saw the man coming towards them, they all, as one, rose and flew in a giant semi-circle, their cries the only sound to be heard in the still morning. Their noise disturbed Oisin's thoughts. He watched the gulls as they turned in the sky ahead of him; then they swooped downwards towards the shoreline, and now twenty or so black and white dots settled once more onto the seaweed to continue feeding. Oisin smiled. He loved the birds. The early morning mist cleared a little and he walked faster now on the hard sand at the water's edge and towards the feeding gulls. His intention had been to head to the spot where so many years ago, he and Bess had stood side by side on that last day, and it was then that he saw the figure in the distance.

He began to feel irritated by the sight of the intruder onto his stretch of sand. His plan had been that he would be alone here in order to collect his thoughts for what lay ahead of him, and, given the early morning and the weather, the figure was unwelcome, but there didn't seem to be any way to avoid the stranger who was now approaching the feeding gulls. The gulls this time remained on the sand, oblivious it seemed, to the oncoming person. This person was now in Oisin's line of vision. He decided that it was a woman's figure because she wore a red and orange floral dress down to her ankles, and that she had lifted a brightly coloured blue and white umbrella over her head and she was busy swinging it around and around, all the while kicking the sand in front of her with bare feet. Given the cold April morning, this seemed to Oisin to be rather foolhardy.

'Hiya,' called the stranger as the two of them were now within speaking distance. Oisin mumbled a greeting and looked away towards the sea.

'Don't remember me?'

She bounded towards him like an over exuberant puppy. Her face was familiar, so familiar, in fact, that he caught his breath.

'Mary?' It couldn't be.

'Thought it was you. They told me you were coming back home. Where have you been all these years? They said you stayed in Australia but no one tells me anything these days. Never a word from anyone. We all thought you were dead.'

'Mary, what are ye doing out here? Ye must be perishin' with the cold.' And he glanced at her bare feet.

'Don't wear shoes on the sand, brother dear.

12

Like to feel the earth beneath my feet. A pagan goddess am I.' She laughed and kicked some sand in his direction. The grains landed on his boots and he frowned. 'No need for clothes most times either. Least not on the beach. You should try it,' she added, twirling the umbrella even faster around her head.

'Where have ye been hiding? Ye came out of nowhere? Thought I had the beach to meself this early morn...?' he asked.

'Oh, here and there... round about... round and round the mulberry bush.'

As if to emphasise her words, she proceeded to twirl the umbrella even faster over her head, and then she threw her head back and let out a high pitched laugh. Hearing the cackle, for that was what it sounded like to Oisin, the gulls on the shoreline rose once again in the air and this time they flew off over the sea.

'Mammy's dying.'

'I know.'

'All the Kelly clan are gathering... and the wanderers return... the waiting begins... and Mammy dies.'

With these words, Mary ran towards the white froth of the waves, and kicked the water in such a violent fashion that the hem of her dress was wet. This was not the action of a rational person and

13

Oisin, somewhat bewildered by what was taking place in front of him and trying so hard to remember his little sister from times past, and happier moments, and now this woman had changed. Why hadn't he been warned? And he wished Claire was beside him for his wife was a straight talking, down-to-earth Aussie, and she would have known what had to be done. Poor Oisin felt quite helpless all of a sudden. Mary, the youngest and the only girl in a family of boys, had been spoilt by them all, mother and father indulged her, everyone did. The last he had heard about Mary was that she made her living as an artist, and a successful one according to family gossip, all the time enjoying the high life in London, and was a well thought of member of the artistic set over the water. He doubted if that description of his little sister would apply to her now. He wondered why she had been wandering along the beach and why at such an early hour but before he had time to ask these questions, Mary turned, folded her umbrella, shoved it into under her left armpit and thrust her face so close to Oisin's that he could smell her breath, stale breath of cigarette smoke, and spat out the words:

'They all hate me, you know... and you're no better. You hate me too.'

Before Oisin had time to defend himself or

reply, she whipped the umbrella from under her arm and thrust the point of it onto his chest. The force of it took his breath away for a second and he stumbled backwards, almost falling into the waves, and in so doing, soaked both his boots and his trousers.

'You're no better than the rest of them, Oisin,' she cried out. And she raised the folded umbrella high above her head. It looked as if she was going to strike her brother with a fury that defied any logical explanation but instead she held the umbrella upright, the offensive weapon now looking like a flagpole, and brother and sister stared at each other, neither knowing quite what to do or say. A few seconds later, she relaxed her tight grip on the umbrella's handle, and looked at Oisin. She was a stranger to him now. Then Mary turned around so that her back was to Oisin, and still holding the umbrella, walked towards the rocks from where he had first noticed her; her head held high and the umbrella resting now upon her left shoulder, marching over the rough white sand like a soldier on parade. He heard her shout over and over, 'Fuck you. And fuck all of Ballybeg too,' until he could hear no more.

CHAPTER TWO

Oisin Kelly was now faced with a dilemma. Meeting his sister, Mary, in such circumstances unsettled him, and the composure he hoped to have before he met with his mother, an arrangement that was due to take place very soon, had all but evaporated to be replaced with worry as to what course of action he should take next. He was a troubled man as he made his way back to An Teach Ban.

There is such a thing as family loyalty, tenuous as it might be in some cases, but for the Kelly family that loyalty held, even if at times it has to be said, by ever such a slight thread. For years the whole family had suffered in varying degrees by the many taunts and false assumptions about their Uncle Mick, 'Mad Mick' as he was called in Ballybeg, and for Oisin to witness his sister's irrational behaviour brought these painful memories back to him. The wall of silence about Mary also worried him. His two brothers had not mentioned her name. It appeared to him now, recalling the conversation of the night before that Mary was no longer part of the Kelly family, a fact that disturbed him as well. As a boy, he had been quite fond of his young sister, spoiling her as much as Frankie and Declan had. The dilemma, it seemed to him, was whether to bring up her name, casually, as a way of finding out more, or to mention that he had met with her on the beach that morning. Neither idea seemed possible, given the anxiety in the house about their mother. He decided to keep quiet about it for the moment and hoped that someone, at some point, perhaps another family member, might enlighten him.

An Teach Ban was full of excitement when he opened the kitchen door to be confronted by Declan's daughter, Mairead and Sean, her two year son. When Mairead, a bubbly young woman of about thirty with a devilish grin and a hair style to match saw Oisin, she threw her arms around him and cried out,

'Ye must be my Uncle Oisin all the way from Australia. To be sure, I never did expect to see ye here in Ballybeg. Da says ye are the one who got away... never to be heard of again... and here ye are. Alive and kickin', so ye are.'

And with that she planted a sloppy kiss onto Oisin's left cheek and hugged him even tighter so that he felt entrapped by her rather large bosom.

'Well, now... ye must be Mairead, Declan's girl. I've been hearin' lots of stories about ye since I've been here. All good, I hasten to add.' He smiled. It was a welcome change to have at least one member of his family happy to see him.

'Have ye heard?' Mairead asked when he was safely inside the kitchen and seated on one of the

17

chairs around the large pine table.

'Heard?'

'Nana. She's sittin' up in bed and asking for ye.'

'For me?'

'Well, it would be, wouldn't it? She sees us all the time. It's you she wants to see. I hope she's goin' to be alright but... she's so old... ?'

There was a pause while Mairead wiped a tear away from her eye. Little Sean rested his curly black head onto his mother's lap. She stroked the boy's hair in a distracted manner, the way a mother does to a young child when her mind is somewhere else, and then she said,

'Nan often talked about ye to me, Uncle Oisin. I think she was... is... proud of

ye and all ye have done,' she grinned. 'Whatever that is?'

This was a surprise to hear. Oisin had always thought his mother preferred Declan, and she was full of pride whenever Frankie's name was mentioned, at least when her eldest son was a priest. Oisin hardly got a mention then. The more Oisin saw in Mairead, the more he began to warm to her. His observant eye noted the devilish humour, and he rather liked that. At times he missed the Irish humour. Australian humour felt different to him, and he had been an outsider no matter how long he had lived there, not quite able

18

to fully grasp the subtleties of his adopted land. He decided he should press Mairead further. Perhaps she might be able to enlighten him as to what had happened to his sister, Mary? But he hesitated. Today was not that sort of day. His mother was asking for him.

'I've thought of my mother too, Mairead,' he said after a few moments had passed. 'We didn't enjoy the best of relationships but I admire her... in so many ways... one of life's survivors is your Gran.'

He had thought of his mother a lot, and even more so these last few weeks when he heard that the end was near, but always her face was the same in his mind; the face of a tired woman who had not shed a tear when he left Ballybeg. Her face would be different now. He was unsure of what sort of face she would have now, so close to death? Maybe, the tiredness would have given way, and this time when she saw him again, she may weep because this was her third son come back to her?

There was a large brown teapot on the table top and fresh scones baked by Joyce that morning. Mairead poured them both a cup of tea and offered Oisin a scone. He was hungry from his walk along the beach and he ate quickly, wiping his mouth on a tissue and drinking the hot tea eagerly. It was the small things you remember, he thought. The brown teapot and the fruit scones and his mother's baking;

his mother, Mick and his young self, him with his short legs swinging under the chair, trying not to eat too many scones for fear of a mother's disapproval, all three of them sitting at the table, talking about nothing in particular.

'I know,' Mairead frowned. She must be thinking of Annie too, Oisin thought. Everyone is thinking of his mother, even his sister, Mary. No one wants to be alone when the last second of life comes.

'Must have been hard, ye know,' Mairead said. 'Can't imagine what it must have been like for her... coming over to Ireland from London... not knowin' what to expect. I think of it sometimes... Nana and her husband and his brother... the three of them all alone at An Teach Ban in those days. Times were so different then. No electricity. No phones. No internet. She must have felt that she had been sent to Siberia, 'specially in the winter when the storms hit the west. But then Nana didn't talk about it much, those early days, an' we used to have long conversations, the two of us. She was my only grandmother after all. Never did meet her mother or my grandfather, Bernard. Nor the famous Uncle Mick,' and Mairead laughed. The mention of Mick always brought either a tear or a chuckle to the family.

'Aye. As the Aussies say, "Annie's a battler", not

surprised she's sittin' up in bed, are ye now?' ' Oisin replied and a picture came into his head of the Annie of his memory.

Mairead laughed. It was just the sort of remark that helped. She decided that she rather liked her Uncle Oisin, and would like to get to know him better, if he stayed around.

'Dad says he'll drive ye into Ballybeg to see Nan. Thinks ye might like to talk to Nan yourself, just the two of you.'

Oisin nodded his head.

'Aye,' he said quietly. 'That might be the best arrangement. Just the two of us.'

****

The memory that Oisin held in his mind for so long about Ballybeg was different from the town that he and his brother, Declan drove through. Changes had come to Ballybeg. It was no longer the sleepy, insular backwater of his childhood. The signpost leading into the town now proudly relayed the message that Ballybeg, Baile Beag, was Ireland's First Eco-town. Declan had met Oisin at the railway station the night before and the familiar streets and houses had been in darkness. Oisin, tired from his long journey, barely noticed the changes but in the daylight everything looked so different. As Declan drove past Murphy's Bar, now converted to a rather spacious up market house, Oisin, struggling in his mind as to what was and what was now, said,

'What's happened to Murphys?' for Murphy's Bar was such a memory for him and he felt a kind of loss, it not being there.

'Sold. After Pa died, Ma sort of lost interest. Hard to believe, I know but there ye go. Young Liam drank himself to death and the other two wouldn't come home so there was no one in the family interested in taking it on. That's life, I guess,' for Declan was always the philosophical one, especially in local matters.

Oisin didn't answer for they were driving along Main Street with the Protestant Church, St Michael's, on the corner with the Manse beside it. But the church had a new life now. A large red sign in Celtic script read: Ballybeg Art Gallery, and the Manse looked to have been given a facelift from his childhood memory, for it certainly was better kept and the gardens were immaculate and looked after. This hadn't been the case when the eccentric Reverend Williamson and his equally eccentric wife, Effie had lived there; funny how he could recall their faces as if it had been yesterday. He made no comment as they sped past and over the North Bridge and across the Owenbeg, now flowing faster thanks to the overnight rain.

Along Main Street, past the library and the Oifig an Phoist, past shops, now painted and prosperous looking, and trendy restaurants with multi-coloured canopies. He caught sight of the spire of St Peter and St Paul, still there, in North Street. The familiarity of it all was seeping into Oisin's mind but the changes were somehow unsettling. But he had changed too. Everything changes after all, and the Ballybeg of his childhood was not the Ballybeg of now. When they turned into Railway Street heading for the hospital, he could feel a kind of anxiety creeping into his consciousness, and he wished Declan would stop talking, just for a moment.

'I'll come in with ye,' announced Declan as they turned into the hospital car park. 'And then leave ye for a while. See how she is today first.'

'I can walk back. Might be good for me to have a look at the old place again. And I've walked home from Ballybeg many the time, have I not?'

'Aye. That we all have,' and Declan smiled.

'Brand new hospital,' said Oisin as they walked along the path towards the hospital entrance and past an ambulance. Two paramedics were there helping an elderly woman into a wheelchair. The woman, hunched over, in pain. A bony hand clung to the wheelchair, and she moaned. The low moan was somehow like a cow in distress. One of the paramedics said, 'C'mon, Bridie, just a few steps

23

more.' But Bridie didn't seem to be able to shuffle just those few steps and the paramedics glanced at each other over the old woman's head. 'Should we get the stretcher?' 'No, Bridie ye can make it, so ye can. Just one more step...' and then Bridie took that one step to tumble ignominiously into the wheelchair. She moaned, louder this time but then the two paramedics got busy. They tucked a shawl around her frail old legs, and wheeled Bridie at speed towards the hospital entrance. Oisin suddenly felt sad.

Declan led the way to their mother's ward. A nurse, carrying a bedpan, smiled at Declan and said,

'Your mother's fine today, Declan. She's had a good night's sleep.'

She glanced at Oisin waiting for an introduction.

'Ah, the wanderer Kelly brother,' the young nurse laughed. 'Now, Annie will be pleased. She's been waitin' for you. Talks about her famous son all the time, you know.'

The nurse was also called Annie. His mother and she had made a connection. The nurse was English too. It was somehow reassuring for Oisin that his mother had an English nurse to look after her in her last days. Life throws up many surprises, and this was one of them. The nurse was not only English; she was a Londoner like Annie.

Annie was propped up on three crisp white pillows with her eyes closed. Declan, always the gentle one, caressed her arm to waken her. Annie's arm was frail and wrinkled and old. She didn't stir. She seemed to be asleep but when Declan kissed her softly on her left cheek, she stirred and opened her eyes. Those blue eyes that once held such a sparkle, now dulled, and Oisin, her third son, felt sad all over again.

'I've brought someone to see ye, Mammy,' and Declan beckoned Oisin to come to their mother's bed.

Annie frowned. She tried to push herself up but she was too weak, and she sank back into the bed.

'It's me, Mammy... Oisin... all the way from Australia...'

'Oisin?'

'Aye, it's me.'

'Can it be? Oisin? Is it really you, Oisin?'

'Aye, Mammy, that it is,' said Declan. 'It's our Oisin an' he's come home to see ye.'

'Well, bless me,' cried Annie. 'I must be dying!'

And the old Annie of Oisin's youth laughed. Declan and Oisin smiled for this was one of those occasions that humour saves the day.

'I'm off now, Mammy,' Declan announced after a few moments. 'Leave you two to catch up.' He grinned at Oisin as he left the ward, and then Oisin and his mother were together for the first time in over forty years. His emotions were all a muddle for in his mind, she was the mother he had said goodbye to, and not the old mother she was now. He still thought of Annie as the brave and energetic woman who held the Kelly family together, despite all their differences. He sat on the bed beside her and took her hand in his. It was her left hand, the flesh around her fingers wrinkled and aged now. This was the hand that had held his. The two wedding rings were still there, side by side on her ring finger. Oisin remembered those rings. One from his father, Bernard, and the other one had come from Uncle Mick. It had been Silvio Luchetta who had brought Mick's ring to Annie so long ago. Annie had kept Mick's ring on her finger, beside his father's wedding ring. Two brothers had loved Annie and she had loved them both. But Annie wanted to talk now. With effort and a sigh, she tried to raise her frail body upwards so that their faces would be closer together. This time she succeeded, and now Oisin and his mother were so close that they could feel each other's breath. Mother and child together once again, for this is a pure bond that is never broken, even if distance and circumstances separate them.

'You know, Oisin,' she whispered, 'I do love all my four children. Every one of you. You're all so different but there's something I want to tell you, Oisin, my dear boy.'

Annie's breathing was uneven. Oisin had to put his head closer to his mother's face in order to hear what she had to say. He made sure it was his good ear as he was now almost totally deaf in the left one.

'Take yer time, Mammy,' he said. He could feel Annie's breath on his cheek.

'There's something I have to tell you, Oisin, my boy... you are the one who always has had my heart.'

Annie sank back onto the pillows, her face beaming. This was a surprise indeed to Oisin. He always thought his mother favoured Declan the most and his ex-priest elder brother, Frankie was the one she was most proud of. Oisin never thought he mattered. But Annie had more she wanted to say.

'You know why you have my heart, Oisin?'

Annie tapped his arm with a bony index finger and now she looked pleased. Oisin shook his head. He was unsure what revelation he was about to hear.

'Because you belong to Mick.'

This was a shock. Oisin frowned, remembering.

'Ye mean... I'm Mick's son?'

His mother laughed. The laughter brought on a cough and it was a few minutes before she was able to speak.

'No, of course not. Oisin, you have to believe

this, son... I was always faithful to your father but Mick, well, your uncle had my heart. I loved him....'

And now Annie wanted to talk. It all came out of her as if she had waited a hundred lifetime's to tell, and through whispers and wheezes, it was to this third son, her Oisin for whom she had waited so long, that she had to unburden her soul. There is nothing harder to bear than locking secrets deep in one's heart, and never being able to speak of them to another living soul. Annie had yearned for this moment, prayed for this moment, and after all those long years, here was her Oisin by her side at last. He heard his mother's confession. No priest could ever have heard such a poignant outpouring in the confessional as Oisin heard that day. Annie held his hand and told him about the night of his conception, how always she had thought Oisin belonged to Mick for she had loved Mick with such intensity that fateful night. And then when Bernard died, the love she felt for her husband's brother became real, and she knew that Oisin had known of this. For in Annie's mind, there was only one person in the whole world who needed to know her secret, and that person was Oisin. Mick had called her son a warrior and a poet, and indeed he had proved to be both.

Annie's eyes shone with a light that was from another dimension in time, and for a precious moment they were not dull anymore. For those few joyful seconds, Annie was in heaven. Oisin didn't speak. His mother stroked his face with a bony hand. He was a little boy again, safe with those hands, and he held Annie's left hand even tighter.

****

There was lightness about Oisin's steps as he made his way along Bridge Street and away from the hospital grounds. His mother's confession had left him reeling for a second or two. In lots of ways, it was the knowledge of the relationship between his mother and Mick that had sent him away from Ballybeg, first to Edinburgh and then to Australia. Mick had been instrumental in this. It was Mick that made sure that the young lad would travel. When Oisin learned of family secrets from the Luchetta family in Edinburgh, he had expanded his horizons away from his beginnings, just as his uncle had predicted that he would. It was also something of admiration for his mother that she had been able to keep all those secrets buried for so long. Sad that there had been no one she felt safe enough to confide in. How many long years she had waited for Oisin to come home? And finally on this day as her life faded away, she could at last release those secrets. Perhaps, for the first time, he loved his mother with unconditional love. Love, after all, is love, he decided, and who was he to judge? In fact, knowing that Mick was Annie's one true love was somehow exciting to him, and after all Oisin, himself, had been in love, but had he ever truly loved? He began to think his mother had been one of the lucky ones. His mother's confession had not only released his mother, it had given Oisin a glimpse of that pure love that exists without judgement, and that had to be a good thing, he concluded.

He decided that he would retrace his childhood by walking around Ballybeg, so rather than walk along the main street which would have been the quickest route, he planned to walk by the side of the Owenbeg, past the boys' school, then to the church of St Peter and Paul. He would then walk the length of Main Street, turn into Railway Street and along to the shore. From then it was just a walk back to North Street, across the North Bridge and then along the road to An Teach Ban.

The day was fine and his spirits were high. He stood for a while at the boys' school and tried not to think of his tormentor-in-chief, Brother Baldy Lawrence whose use of the strap on Oisin, the memory of which still made him angry. When the beatings came, Oisin was a mirror of his Uncle Mick. Both stoic and defiant, neither would flinch.

The school was quiet. It was Saturday and there were no boys in the playground, just two seagulls tugging at some leftover bread. Each bird was doing the very best to pull all the food into its beak. They were evenly matched and neither seemed willing to give up until the stronger one, a larger bird, managed to grab all the food and flew off in the direction of the Owenbeg. The smaller bird, now in a fury, chased its rival and the two birds continued their fight over the river until the stronger one, now showing signs of exhaustion, dropped all the food into the river. The smaller bird swooped down and retrieved the leftover bread and then, still screeching, the two birds flew off together. Oisin watched the dispute with interest. His long years in the Australian outback had taught him the wisdom that can come from just being able to stop and stare and observe the natural world. The seagulls amused him. Others might have passed by and not even noticed the drama but Oisin was not one of those. He had the soul of a poet.

His attention was drawn to the school buildings which looked much the same as he remembered; a newer and larger building than the original classrooms had been added, so the school was now L-shaped. No doubt a larger building was necessary to house the expanding population of Ballybeg. The playground was smaller. He wondered if the boys had enough room there to play and if they tried to escape over the wall to the fields beyond the river. He had often played truant, disappearing for a few hours and sometimes for a day. He had been glad to leave the place. It held no happy memories.

The church held no happy memories either. Times change and he had changed as well. People fear change, he thought, but nothing remains as it was. St Peter and St Paul's was just as imposing a building as ever but it was a building after all. It was the people who worshipped there who changed.

It was when he turned into the main street that he became aware of more changes. The town seemed busy with people hurrying about. He didn't recognise anyone. There was brashness about Ballybeg now. It was no longer the sleepy inward-looking community of his youth. Maybe it was something about becoming an eco-town and famous. He wondered what his father and Mick would have made of the place. Neither would have been pleased, he thought, eco-town or not. Shops he remembered were no longer there. The bakery where he used to spend his pocket money on sticky buns was a mobile phone shop now. He passed an internet café and a book shop. McNally's pub had been transformed into a smart looking restaurant called *The Green Leprechaun*. The outside walls were covered in bottle green. There was a painted wooden figure of a leprechaun at the door. The little man held a blackboard with today's specials chalked on it. Oisin began to despair.

He strolled at a leisurely pace up the hill along the main street, past oak benches, shops now bright and cheerful and a line of trees with iron railings around them, all these things designed to emphasise the fact that Ballybeg was eco-friendly. All the time he took note of his surroundings as was his nature. He began to feel hungry. Declan had insisted that they arrive at the hospital early as he said Annie was usually better in the morning and more coherent. She would be able to take in the fact that Oisin was there. Later on in the day, she might not be so alert. So Oisin hadn't eaten for hours and now he looked around for somewhere to have a light lunch. There was plenty of choice. Restaurants and coffee lounges seemed to more in evidence than the pubs of old. He finally decided on one place at the corner of Main Street and Railway Street.

He remembered the building used to house the *Ballybeg News,* much read by his father and uncle. A transformation had taken place. He recalled how he used to collect the paper for his father after school and how the place had been untidy, dirty and noisy with a rather churlish printer and an equally rude reporter in attendance. The two men didn't like the Kellys, and in particular, Mick, and neither of them spoke when the young Oisin picked up the weekly paper, just handed it to him with not so much as a grunt. Now the place was bright and inviting, renamed *The Cat and the Fiddle*. A lively young red-haired waitress escorted him to a table next to the cappuccino machine and handed him the menu. *The Cat and the Fiddle* was busy. Oisin looked around to see about twenty or so posters and some framed prints of cats, all different shapes, colours and sizes with an actual fiddle tacked onto the wall amongst all these cats and, taking pride of place in the centre, a giant poster of a black and white cat playing a fiddle. It was all very imaginative and inviting although Oisin wondered what cats had to do with coffee but then, this was the new Ballybeg after all. On the opposite wall, next to where Oisin sat, there were posters of various sizes, some brightly coloured and others black and white, and all of them very twenty-first century, Save the Siberian Tiger, Climate Change, Pollution, Save the Amazon Rainforest; and at the counter next to the cappuccino machine, a hand printed sign which read NO PLASTIC HERE. Oisin felt quite at home. It was a much friendlier place than the old newspaper office. He ordered a spinach and ricotta pasta topped with pine nuts and a crusty white bread roll for lunch. The red haired waitress was busy but she gave Oisin a friendly smile of welcome when she took his order.

He enjoyed his meal and asked for a large cup of cappuccino. It was then that he noticed a man about his own age sitting at the table underneath the poster of the cat and the fiddle. The man kept staring at him. The man looked familiar but Oisin couldn't think of his name until the stranger came to his table and asked could he sit down?

'Do ye remember me?' the stranger asked a puzzled Oisin. 'A year below ye at the Christian Brothers.... Seamus O'Maera?'

'Sure, now I remember ye, Seamus. We've put many a year behind us since then. Sit yeself down.'

Oisin did remember Seamus. Seamus, the scrawny kid whose mother, a widow with six children to raise on her own, and who had decided that Seamus, her eldest, should be a priest, as did Brother Baldy and Father O'Malley, and just about everyone, except, that is, Seamus. For the scrawny kid had decided that he wanted to be a nurse and nothing and no one was going to stop him. Seamus O'Maera was no longer scrawny. Most of his hair had gone, and he had filled out somewhat, especially around the waist, but his dark blue eyes still had the same twinkle that Oisin remembered. Oisin, not fitting into the mould at school either, admired Seamus for all the same reasons.

'I'm retiring this year,' announced Seamus.

'Twenty-five years I've been at the Ballybeg Hospital and loved every minute of it.'

'Ye become a nurse, after all,' said Oisin with a grin.

'Aye, against all the odds. How about ye? Heard ye went to Australia and made quite a name of yeself out there.'

'Who said that?'

'Ye mother, of course. Been looking after Annie for months now. Sure, she's a grand woman, yer mammy. One of the best. And she doesn't half sing your praises.'

Oisin was silent, thinking of his mother and the morning's confession.

'I came home to see her... forty years it's been since I left Ballybeg... they tell me she hasn't got long, that's why I'm here.'

'Well, she'll be at peace now, Oisin, God rest her. We all thought she was waitin' for ye.'

'I didn't think I was that important to her.'

'Ah, Oisin, me lad, ye always were a modest fellow, now, weren't ye?'

He looked around.

'And, now tell me, what do ye think of the new Ballybeg... the eco-town? Can ye believe that this old place is now the best coffee lounge in town? Far cry from the *Ballybeg News,* and those miserable buggers that used to be in here.'

'Sure, it's for the best, Seamus, there's no doubt about it. What a change... used to dread comin' in to get the paper for ma Da. By the way, where can I get a copy of *The Ballybeg News,* just out of interest?'

'No paper copies any more. This is an eco-town, zero waste. Ye get an app.'

'Oh.'

The two men grinned.

'They're closing Main Street to cars in a few weeks' time too. Been talking about it for years. A few of them on the Council want Ballybeg to be car-free but I can't see that happening. It's all this eco thing, ye know. Changes. All change. Some good, some not so good but that's life, I guess. Don't know what the old ones make of it all.' He grinned. 'And we're getting' to be the old folks now, aren't we, Oisin me lad?' Seamus got up.

'Well, good to see ye again, Oisin.' And he held out his hand. 'Suppose ye know about yer sister, Mary?'

'Mary?'

'Aye. Didn't anyone tell ye? She's a regular visitor to the Ballybeg Hospital.'

'What do ye mean, Seamus?'

'Ah. Well, Mary's like the dark side of the moon, and that's when we meet her. Other times, well, she's the light side, and that's the Mary we all want to see. I'm sorry, Oisin. It's been hard on your family, seeing Mary's dark side and knowing there's nothing anyone can do. We do our best for her but yer sister's not well, Oisin. Just thought ye knew.'

Oisin, who a few moments before had been quite elated, now could see his sister and the madness in her eyes. He could hear Mary's angry words. He felt the umbrella end piercing his chest. He wished Seamus hadn't been the one to tell him. The two men said goodbye outside the coffee lounge but it was a thoughtful Oisin who made his way back along Railway Street towards the sea, and the bench where his mad Uncle Mick used to sit, watching the waves.

CHAPTER THREE

When Oisin arrived back at An Teach Ban it was already dark. There was a surprise awaiting him. He had taken a long and leisurely walk from Ballybeg, and was feeling rather pensive. When he opened the door he was greeted by Declan's wife, Joyce. She took hold of his arm and whispered into his good ear,

'Oisin, you have a visitor.' She looked flustered as if this particular visitor wasn't entirely welcome

In the short time that he had been back at An Teach Ban, Oisin had become rather fond of Joyce. She was a kind woman and fussed over him, in the nicest possible way. He judged that his brother had made a good choice in his marriage as Declan and Joyce seemed compatible, at least from an outsider's point of view. Joyce, the Englishwoman from Hastings, had settled into life in the west of Ireland in a comfortable sort of way. She appeared to be liked by everyone, because when Oisin mentioned her name, the response was always positive. His English mother, Annie, had had much more difficulty becoming part of the small community. But then, times were different and this generation travelled and were slightly more tolerant of newcomers, especially the English.

Joyce was an understanding woman. When

Oisin told her a little of his near death experience in the woodshed at Wiesenthal, and how the blows that Hans Seefeldt had given him then, blows which had resulted in the loss of hearing in the left ear, she nodded her head and assured him that she would make sure he heard her when she spoke. From then on, she remembered to avoid his left ear. Oisin, who over the years had finally lost most of the hearing in that ear, appreciated this small act of kindness. So the news there was a visitor to see him was a surprise, only Joyce didn't look too pleased as to who this particular visitor was.

The visitor was dressed in a tweed skirt and a heavy embroidered woollen cardigan with reindeers and Christmas trees, even though it was April and Christmas was a long way away. She wore purple tights and heavy brown leather shoes. Her grey hair was tied up in a bun. A huge tortoiseshell hair clip kept hair away from her eyes which were heavily made up with blue eyeshadow, black eyeliner and even darker mascara. A dark red lipstick covered her lips so that when she threw her arms around Oisin and kissed him, there was a perfect transfer of red onto his cheek. Oisin stepped back, somewhat embarrassed. The visitor was his sister, Mary.

'My dear, dear big brother,' she cried out. 'It's been so long...'

A small tear appeared under all the eye makeup and ran down her cheek. She wouldn't let him go. Her arms were strong and Oisin tried to move away but she held him tight. All the time Joyce looked at them. The small kitchen all of a sudden seemed crowded with emotion. This wasn't the Mary of yesterday when Oisin had been sworn at, and stabbed with an umbrella.

'Well now,' Oisin finally released, sat down at the pine table, unable to quite grasp what was happening.

Then Mary started to talk. It seemed she wasn't able to stop for the words tumbled out and her voice grew louder. She was theatrical. She strode round and round the table, pushing Joyce aside as she did. The tortoiseshell cat fled to the next room. Mary, who a second or two had greeted Oisin in the way of a long lost relative, now completely ignored him. She set about putting the world to rights, at least in a political way, and it was the politicians and the global capitalists who received the most venom. She spoke of Che Guevara as if he had been a personal friend. Oisin decided that his sister's ramblings boarded on the manic. Both Oisin and his sister-in-law, Joyce were at a loss as to what to do until all of a sudden, Mary turned on Joyce,

'Haven't you any opinion, Joyce?' she snapped. 'Or are you one of those women who meekly accept

41

their lot in life and have no thought of anything in the world except cooking meals and mending their husband's clothes?'

The gentle Joyce blushed, as if the words were daggers that drew blood. She looked to Oisin for help but for once, none came. Oisin was speechless, which was unusual for him because he could always been counted on for an opinion, or at least, some good old banter. The shock of the Mary on the beach and the Mary in the kitchen was just too much for him, coming on top of his rather traumatic day.

'Women like you are a disgrace,' Mary spat out. 'Stand up for yourself, why don't you?'

Mary took a cigarette out of her cardigan pocket and lit it even though she knew Joyce disapproved of smoking. She blew some smoke in the direction of Joyce and Joyce coughed.

Now Mary turned on Oisin. She draped her arm around his shoulders. All the time she held the lit cigarette perilously close to his face. He moved his head away to avoid both the smoke and also the proximity of Mary. He could smell stale whiskey on her breath.

'You agree with me, don't you, Oisin? Joyce should stand up for herself.'

'I... can't really comment on this, Mary. I've just met Joyce, after all,' and Oisin smiled at Joyce, to give both reassurance and kindness.

But Mary was relentless. Didn't Joyce know that she was a doormat to her brother, Declan? That Declan was like all men, selfish and thoughtless? Joyce did all the work around the house, as well as keeping all the holiday cabins clean and tidy. This new enterprise might be prospering but it was all due to the work of Joyce who never complained, and for this reason alone, she was a doormat. By this time Mary had left Oisin's side and now she circled the table. As her voice rose, so did her movement. She waved her arms and pointed at Joyce, who by this time was endeavouring as best she could to keep out of the way. Mary was incandescent, imagining all manner of injustices that the passive Joyce suffered at the hands of her alleged aggressive husband. Until exhausted, Mary slumped into the kitchen chair, next to the bewildered Oisin. She lit another cigarette and smiled at her sister-in-law as if nothing had happened.

'I'm sorry, Joyce,' she said. 'Really I am. It's just that I believe strongly in the rights of women and you seem to me to be oblivious to our struggle. I don't want to think that the suffragettes have died for nothing.'

Then she turned to Oisin, and said in a clear voice, devoid of all emotion,

"Have you a wife, Oisin?'

'Ye must know that I have, Mary. Been married to Claire for thirty-two years... or is it thirty-three, thirty-four... can never remember dates. Claire's always reminding me on many occasions.'

'No one bothered to tell me any of this. Didn't even know you were married. That's what this family is like. It's as if I don't exist. No one tells me anything. What's she like, your Claire?'

'She puts up with me. Well, Claire's a real Aussie battler. Calls a spade a spade, does Claire.'

He wondered what Claire would make of his sister and how they would get on. They wouldn't, he thought. No way would Claire put up with any theatricals and she would have been horrified at Mary's treatment of Oisin on the beach; she'd have given Mary a piece of her mind, so she would. But then, maybe Mary is in that dark place, the dark side of the moon, like Seamus said. Maybe she needs help, not judgement.

The friction in the room was broken at that moment. Declan opened the door and strode in. He took off his coat and hung it on the peg next to Mick's old leather chair. Declan was the peacemaker of the family. He saw his wife's face, looked at Mary, then to Oisin, and decided to diffuse the situation with some humour.

'My word, Mary, my dear,' he said, 'aren't ye lookin' grand tonight, so ye are. Sure, ye don't look

44

a day over twenty in that outfit. Now then, what's that yer wearin'? Looks like Christmas has arrived early here, so.' And he grinned at the woollen cardigan with reindeers and Christmas trees.

This sudden change of conversation seemed to please Mary. In fact, she laughed. She left Oisin and clasped Declan in a huge embrace. Over his sister's head, Declan smiled at Joyce. The tension in the kitchen eased and Oisin breathed a sigh of relief. Joyce now was able to busy herself with the evening meal. She seemed grateful for the task. Oisin noticed that Joyce avoided looking in Mary's direction. When she served Mary's meal, she seemed to keep her distance but she hovered over Declan and Oisin, and repeatedly asked them if they would not like some more potatoes, or stew? Oisin, forever the observer, noticed the body language between the two women. A less aware person wouldn't even have detected this hesitancy on Joyce's part to come close to Mary. But it was a lot calmer family who sat down at the table.

'How was Mammy today, Oisin?' asked Declan when the meal was finished and all four relaxed, even Mary, who hadn't spoken a word.

'She was at peace, I think. Aye, that's what she was... at peace.'

'Ah. I knew it. She's been waitin' for ye, Oisin. She hung on until she saw ye again.' He looked sad.

'Aye. I think ye are right,' replied Oisin in his quiet way. 'Mammy is happy now.' And he thought of Mick.

****

Every day Annie grew weaker. Sometimes when Oisin sat by her bed, she talked about all the old times, of London and her mother and jovial Uncle George, and Ballybeg as it used to be. But now her stories were rambling ones and hard to follow, and even harder to understand. Annie's breathing was laboured. She told Oisin she just wanted to close her eyes. Mick and Bernard were waiting for her in heaven. She slept more than she was awake. Oisin held her hand then. It was a connection between the two of them that he had not felt for so long, and now there was sadness in his heart. It had taken him many years to come home to Ireland, to An Teach Ban, but then life got in the way, and he never thought that his mother had cared for him anyway. So he kept away and got on with his own life and Kilgoolga had become his home. But now seeing his mother and hearing what she told him, he knew he had always had her love, and he was glad.

He began to wonder how long he should stay with his brother and sister-in-law at An Teach Ban. His elder brother, Frankie and his wife, Ellen had already gone back to Dublin to wait for news of any change. Oisin thought maybe he should do likewise. At least, stay in Ireland but not too far away. He didn't know quite what to do for the best. His life seemed to be full of everyone else's problems at the moment. It was true that his sister Mary had unsettled him most of all. He tried to find some way to understand how Mary had changed from the kid who used to follow him around to the woman she now was. Then perhaps he could make some sense of it. After all, she is ill and mental illness is something no one wants to talk about, even now, he decided. The human mind is unfathomable. What had happened in Mary's life, he wondered as he sat by his mother's bed side? How much does Annie know about her daughter's mental state? Surely, that couldn't have been kept from her for any length of time. But then he didn't know how long Mary had been ill. No one wanted to talk about it. When one member of a family can't cope with life, often the others close ranks and don't speak about it; a sense of shame seems to descend upon everyone. It was like a cloak of darkness that came like a demon and enveloped them all. He began to think his own family had done just that. No one had mentioned Mary's name in any letters or emails that he had received in Kilgoolga. He thought she was living in London and a successful artist. At least, that was what he had assumed because that was the last he had heard about his sister. Now he began to wonder. Truth matters, he thought but then, everyone's interpretation of that truth can vary? Declan, for instance, might see Mary in a different way and his interpretation would be different. And as for Joyce, why did Mary hate her so much? What did Joyce make of Mary's antagonism towards her? He decided the best person to approach would be Joyce. At least, Joyce wasn't a blood member of the Kelly family, and for that reason would be able to distance herself from the familial bond somewhat. At least, that's what he hoped.

****

Oisin's dilemma about his sister was further thwarted by the reticence of Joyce to talk about it. He had been rather cautious when he brought up the subject of Mary, not wishing to pry but curious as to what had been happening in the years he had been away. Joyce was vague in her reply and frustratingly so. Whatever was between the two women, it appeared that's where it would remain. Oisin would not find out anything from Joyce.

A few days later, he was out walking along the road towards the next farm where old Mother Fahy and her handicapped son had lived. The old lady was long gone and the son had been taken to a home to be cared for. No one knew what had happened to him but the general assumption was that, he too, had died. Old Mother Fahy had left the farm to a distant cousin in Tipperary who had been relieved when their neighbour, Declan Kelly put in an offer that could not be refused. Oisin had not met with Declan's son, Ryan but from all accounts, he was the apple of his mother's eye and a hero to his father. Ryan was in his early forties and lived with his girlfriend, a doctor, Alice Geraghty. Apparently neither Ryan nor Alice had any desire for either marriage or children and for those reasons, did not quite fit into the mould that Ballybeg folk liked people to be in, and the two of them were therefore left to their own devices. Even if it was the twenty-first century and social mores had changed somewhat, the old ways still were there in many minds, and especially in Annie's. Ryan's grandmother had not approved of the relationship and had been quite vocal in her displeasure in the beginning. But Ryan and Alice had lived together for nearly twelve years, and Annie finally, and somewhat reluctantly, came to accept that they would never marry, and there would be no grandchildren. So Oisin, always having felt an outsider as well, was curious to meet his nephew. It would appear that at least two members of the Kelly clan had not wanted to fit into a particular mould.

Ryan was a farmer, like his father. He farmed free range chickens; the eggs he sold to his mother for the farm shop and the surplus went to the shops in Ballybeg. It had been an excellent move, given that Ballybeg was now an eco-town and fresh local produce was much desired. Ryan had also built six holiday cabins on the land. Similar in design to the ones at An Teach Ban the cabins were set high on the hillside, away from the house and with an enviable view looking towards the sea. The cabins were comfortable, all with a porch in the front of them and a gravel track outside for cars. There was one large cabin which catered for six people. The remaining five were two bedroom affairs with an open plan kitchen and sitting room and a bathroom at the back. The cabins were comfortable, clean and cosy. His parents at An Teach Ban had converted an outbuilding to a communal kitchen and spacious living area but Ryan had no such aspirations. His holiday cottages were advertised as 'a getaway' from it all. People could wander down to An Teach Ban or Ballybeg if they couldn't live without the internet. Added to the rural idyll a gaggle of nine geese patrolled the property. The geese were particular favourites of Ryan, a vegetarian. The fortunate geese were therefore destined to live a comfortable life to old age. In one of these cabins, set somewhat apart from the others, lived Ryan's Aunt Mary but no one in the family had bothered to mention this fact to Oisin.

****

Old Mother Fahy's cottage bore no resemblance to the cottage of Oisin's memory. Gone was the ancient, thatched roof to be replaced with grey slates. Just two very basic rooms had been the cottage of Oisin's memory but now the dwelling was lengthier and looked very well cared for. Old Mother Fahy had survived on a dirt floor. There was double glazed windows and central heating in this house now. Oisin brushed past the purple, fuchsia bushes which grew in profusion either side of a brightly painted red door and rang the bell. A few moments later the door opened and a tall thin man with a black beard and hair to his shoulders greeted him.

'Ye must be my Uncle Oisin, all the way from Australia,' the man with the curly hair said. 'I've heard many reports about ye, so I have. Da said ye might drop in. C'mon in and sit yeself down. The kettle's just boiled. Would ye be havin' some tea? Or maybe something stronger?'

'Tea will be just fine. Bit early in the day for anything stronger,' answered Oisin, as he followed

Ryan along the hallway and into the kitchen.

Ryan was tall and thin like all the Kellys. He swayed slightly as he walked, and following behind him, Oisin thought that his nephew's gait was similar to a rather large Emperor penguin swaying from side to side. Oisin wondered if Ryan had suffered an injury to his hips some time in his life. But then, even if he had, he doubted if anyone in his family would have bothered to tell him. After all, no one had mentioned Mary.

When Ryan entered the kitchen he turned and smiled at Oisin. His brown eyes did not come from the Kellys, but from his mother, Joyce, and they were kind eyes. Oisin felt the warmth of those eyes as he sat down at the kitchen table in the room that he never thought he would ever see again. But it wasn't the room of his memory. There was nothing of Old Mother Fahy or her unfortunate son anywhere for the transformation of a house was complete; no blue and white dresser with the lines of willow pattern plates, and the Virgin Mary and baby Jesus no longer held pride of place on the wall next to the dresser. That was the humble dwelling of old. This was a different time and a different home. Painted off white walls, brightly patterned curtains covering a window that wasn't there before, and the large cream Aga now stood where the dresser used to be, giving warmth and comfort to this cheery room. A very large black and brown dog of mixed parentage stood up, stretched his front legs, arched his back and yawned. The dog acknowledged the presence of the two men in the room with one tired woof; then he slowly walked towards Oisin who patted the top of the dog's head as a way of saying hello. The dog responded with a quick sniff of Oisin's hand, and then he mooched off to lie once more on the rug not far from the warmth of the Aga.

'That's Jasper,' said Ryan to introduce the dog. 'He's an old boy now. Just wants to sleep, don't you, Jasper?'

Jasper opened one sleepy eye, wagged the tip of his rather bushy dark brown tail, closed both eyes, and in a matter of seconds, gentle snores came from his open mouth. This welcome distraction meant that Oisin relaxed while Ryan busied himself pouring hot water from a large kettle into a decorated ceramic teapot. Watching him, Oisin had a flashback of memory, and it was Old Mother Fahy making the tea for him on his last visit to her all those years ago, and the gift of the silver eggcup that she insisted that he keep as a going away present, for wasn't he off to America like so many of the poor Irish? He had kept the eggcup and he had that memory. Sitting there, he felt at home, even more at home than at An Teach Ban if the truth be told.

Life has many surprises and this was one of them. He took a bite from an oatcake that Ryan had set before him and sipped his tea.

'Never thought I'd be in this room again,' he said between chews. 'I was fond of Old Mother Fahy but she sure lived in a hovel.'

'Never met her myself,' answered Ryan. He looked thoughtful. 'It was Da that bought the farm after the old lady passed away. I wanted to be a farmer and ma Da saw an opportunity. I moved around a bit and when I was twenty-five, I came back to Ballybeg and the rest is history, so they say. Saw a bit of the world I did, never got to Australia though, I'd have looked ye up if I had. Then I met Alice a few years later. Best thing that ever happened to me, meeting Alice, and taking over Old Mother Fahy's farm, the icing on the cake for me. I'll show ye round if ye like, after we finish our tea.'

Oisin nodded. Ryan was another generation. He felt old all of a sudden. He thought everyone had known Old Mother Fahy but then, he'd been away for forty years.

'I'd like to do that,' he replied. 'Believe ye have lots of chickens and plenty of eggs to sell. Heard all this from your mother.'

'Aye. And the log cabins to rent to the tourists. The Kellys have branched out.'

'I've noticed.'

'Well, we saw the writing on the wall for the farming. Da always has had an eye for business and the way things looked to be going, it was a natural progression. The cabins were all Ma's idea. She comes from Hastings in England and knew how to cater for the tourists. She told us that we have the best views in the world after all, and there's a lot of weary city folk to cater for. Years ago ye couldn't survive on the view but now, the view is everything. Things turn around.'

'Aye. That they do.'

'When Ballybeg became an eco-town a few years back, we knew we were on to a winner. But we'd decided on the cabins and filling them with arty types and tourists before then. Could be said that the Kellys were ahead of the game on this one.'

They finished their tea and Ryan got up. He steadied himself slightly on the edge of the table. *This man has injured himself at some time*, thought Oisin. He had seen enough of people's injuries and suffered his own pain as well. He contemplated asking his nephew about his legs, then thought better of it for Ryan was already calling for him. When Oisin followed Ryan into the yard, nine geese joined them, waddling behind Ryan in single file so that Oisin became part of the small procession.

'They think I'm their father,' said Ryan as a way of explanation. 'They're a great attraction for the visitors although sometimes they can cause a bit of a fuss, especially with some city folk who have a fear of anything with feathers that honks.' Hearing Ryan's voice, all nine lifted their collective heads, and honked loudly, making quite a racket until Ryan shooed them away with a wave of his hand. Then they all wobbled off in the direction of a patch of grass and were soon eating away, leaving a trail of green and dark brown excrement behind them. The sight of the geese amused Oisin. He judged they would be ideal guard dogs, given that old Jasper appeared to spend his days asleep in front of the fire. There didn't seem to be any other dogs about.

'They seem to respond to you, sure... it's a father's command... works every time... well, that's the theory,' Oisin said with a grin, and he thought of his own daughter, Suze who hardly ever took any notice of him and had always gone her own way, just like his wife, Claire. Maybe the nine geese were female?

The view took Oisin's breath away for here was the west in all its grandeur, and even if the outlook from An Teach Ban was so familiar to him, even now, and magical in its own way; here the sea was just a few metres away and the mountain of so many dreams, Slieve Geal loomed behind them, its cone-like shape now covered in a light mist. The mountain was nature's protector. All the childhood years Oisin had spent beside it, he had never climbed it from Old Mother Fahy's place. Now he had such a desire to clamber up its rocky sides and stand at the very top, breath in the air of his homeland and be grateful for his life and what he had done. Soft rain landed on his face and hair like droplets of dew. This was the Ireland of imagination and sweet memories. Wispy white clouds strung out in lines across the soft blue sky, some of them were now darkening as more rain seemed imminent. With his good ear, he could just make out the crashing of the waves on the rocks, those rocks where he had stood just a few days before with his sister, Mary.

'I would like to climb Slieve Geal from here,' he said to Ryan, 'before I leave.'

He felt he was giving himself a promise, and if he said the words aloud, he would make it happen and not let any thoughts of age or infirmity get in his way. Ryan seemed to understand the significance of his uncle's remark for he nodded his head and replied that he, too, would like to climb with him although the shale at the very top of the mountain would make it a challenge for them both.

'My legs need a bit of help since the accident,' Ryan said.

'My hearing needs a bit of help these days, as well. I tell people to shout into my right ear, my left one's no good now.'

'I'll remember that,' answered Ryan with a slight grin.

'What happened to your legs?' asked Oisin for in such a short space of time, he had become a friend to his nephew, and a direct question wouldn't offend.

'I was in a car accident in Italy. Set off on the journey of a lifetime, all by myself and my trusty VW campervan. Well, the trusty old VW ran off the road near Bologna on a sharp bend. I tried to miss a truck piled high with cabbages; I remember, and hit a tree instead. I ended up in the hospital out there for six months. I broke my pelvis and they had to put two pins into each of my hips. It was all a bit tricky as I didn't know the language but there was a doctor there who spoke English and patched me up so I could walk again but I still feel a bit of pain now and then in my legs. Climbing can be difficult these days but I'd like to try to get to the top of the old mountain with ye. Be a challenge that it would.'

He smiled. 'Anyway I'm OK most of the time. Maybe that's why I found a doctor to look after me here. Ye know that Alice's a GP in Ballybeg?'

'Aye. Your mother told me about Alice.'

The two men were silent for a few moments, both with their memories. Ryan's memories of that time in the Italian hospital still held pain.

'Aye. I'll always remember that young doctor in Italy... now what was her name again... ? Aye, that's right, Doctor Luchetta.'

'Luchetta? I knew a family called Luchettas once, in Edinburgh. Silvio Luchetta came to Ballybeg a lot. He knew Uncle Mick.'

'Well now, I didn't know that. Doubt if they would be any relation. Guess Luchetta is a common name in Italy.'

'Aye. Ye are probably right, Ryan. Would be too much of a coincidence, wouldn't it now?'

But Oisin wondered, even as he said the words. He hadn't thought of Silvio Luchetta or any of the Luchetta family in years. Hearing their name again brought back a rather special time he had had with them, but then there was Cecy, and he hadn't thought of her for years either. He decided to talk of other things to keep the memories out of his head. He had been in love with Cecy after all.

'Do ye want to show me around your Estate... before those clouds up there turn to more rain?' he asked his nephew as a way of changing the subject. He didn't want to talk about the Luchettas he had known, not now, perhaps not ever. And no one knew about Cecy, not even his wife, Claire. No one, but Eleanor Bradshaw and she was dead.

It became evident within a matter of seconds that Ryan possessed a reverence for all living

59

creatures and those living creatures, in turn, responded in such a way as to suggest that their response to him was not totally because of the food and shelter that he provided for them because when he introduced Oisin to the two donkeys, Bella and Bertha, for instance, the two animals greeted him with enthusiastic he-haws as only donkeys can, and appeared genuinely pleased to see their owner. The two donkeys followed the men around the perimeter of the fence and stood looking rather forlorn when Ryan disappeared towards the hen run with Oisin following behind him. A similar thing happened with the chickens. Although Ryan kept fifty or so brown hens for their eggs, he also had various other poultry breeds around the place. These lucky hens wandered freely and followed Ryan in much the same way as the geese had done so now there was a selection of assorted chickens, Sussex, Marans, bantams of various colours and two flighty little Seabright hens, one black speckled and the other one, brown, all clucking away around Ryan.

'Ye would be surprised how many city kids don't know where eggs come from, Oisin,' Ryan said as he threw a handful of grain onto the ground towards the favoured gang of hens. 'Some of them think in all seriousness that eggs arrive in cartons from the supermarket, and it's a surprise for them when they hear that milk doesn't come in a plastic bottle. Sad state of affairs.'

Oisin could only agree with this statement.

They walked past a fenced off area which had been made into a vegetable garden. Here winter cabbages and swedes were still in the ground. Part of the garden had been dug up ready for the spring planting and Oisin wondered at the energy Ryan must have to look after all of this. As if he read his mind, Ryan told me that he did have assistance around the place, especially in the summer when the visitors came. He employed a lad from Ballybeg who helped look after the hens and the other animals, and in the summer backpackers arrived, mostly French and German students, who all seemed to be fascinated by the history of Ireland and the Irish. Something about Ryan's quiet optimism pleased Oisin and he said as much.

'Oh, well, Uncle Oisin. That's life,' Ryan replied. 'It's good to have young faces around. All that energy. Keeps me fit, ye know, and I have my Da for the wisdom that comes with age to call on if needed. Well, that's what I keep tellin' the old man.' And he chuckled.

'Talking of age,' he continued, 'I don't think Nana will be coming home to An Teach Ban, do ye?'

Oisin shook his head.

'Guess ye will want to stay for a while then?'

Ryan asked.

'Aye. That I will. I want to be with her till the end... I owe her that much.'

The two men walked on, both of them were thinking of Annie and what she had been.

At one of the cabins Ryan stopped and opened the door. It was cosy inside with a log burner and a pile of firewood beside it. He said,

'Ye are welcome to stay here if ye need a bit of peace from An Teach Ban. We can't let this cabin out yet... needs a bit of repair work to the roof but it's water tight.

What do ye think?'

Oisin wondered if this might be a good offer. He had been finding being with Declan and Joyce and the constant stream of visitors a little wearisome these last few days. Maybe a bit of solitude might be what he needed. After all, Ryan's cabins were advertised as a 'get away from it all'. He thought of the solitude that the empty spaces of the outback in Kilgoolga gave him. Perhaps he was missing all that. People were all very good but space is often needed to recharge the soul.

'Aye,' he said. 'I'd like that. I could help ye with any repairs needed. Been thinking that I've been getting under your mother's feet a bit lately... An Teach Ban is a bit like Central Station sometimes.'

'Aye.'

The two men walked back towards the house in silence. Words, even between friends, could intrude sometimes and this was one of those times. The fine rain had turned heavier. It looked like the day was set to be a rainy one. Above the wispy line of white clouds had given way to dark cumulus ones and the sky was no longer blue, but darkening. This sudden change of light and atmosphere was something that Oisin had missed for so long. Most of the year, living in outback Kilgoolga there was nothing but blue sky. When he left, it hadn't rained for eighteen months and the farmers were weary. He quite understood why the Irish miss the rain when they leave their Emerald Isle.

Oisin thought he saw a shadowy figure at the window as they passed the last log cabin. This cabin was a little apart from the rest and situated on a slight slope.

'Have ye guests already in that cabin?' He asked Ryan as they passed. It seemed a bit strange to him as there had been no evidence of occupancy in the other cabins. A few moments before Ryan had mentioned that the season hadn't started yet. Normally the bookings started in late April through till early winter. It gave everyone a chance to get the cabins ready for the guests to arrive if they closed for the five months of winter, and it was a welcome break for all. Ryan didn't seem to hear the question so Oisin asked him again.

'Aye,' Ryan answered after another few moments. 'That particular cabin is booked all year.'

'That's good.'

'Well, I'm not sure of that.'

'Why's that?'

'Mary's lives there... '

'Mary? My sister, Mary?'

'Aye. That's the one.'

'I thought she lived in London... '

'Aye. That she did... until the illness... thought someone might have told ye.'

'I've not heard a word.' And Oisin remembered again Mary on the beach and the umbrella stabbing him in the chest. It was just a few minutes' walk from Ryan's place to the beach where he had met his sister. Now he understood how she had got there and how quickly she had departed from him.

'Guess someone should have mentioned it to ye but ye being so far away, sort of thing. Alice and I decided to let her live there especially after what she did to my mother. Seemed the best solution all round and Alice, being a GP, could keep an eye on her. Well, Mary's in and out of the hospital and needs to stay on her medication to keep her on the safe and narrow. We hardly see her. She only makes an appearance when she's on the upward slope but we've all learned to cope with it, I guess. Da and

Mammy find it hard though, especially Mammy.'

'What happened, Ryan? If ye want to tell me, that is.'

Ryan nodded his head. He seemed sad and Oisin wondered just what had happened to make him decide to offer Mary a home.

'Let's go back into the house first, Oisin. Get out of the rain.'

The sunny day had now changed in the dramatic way that happens in the west and as more black clouds gathered overhead, the wind direction had altered as well. The gentle raindrops of the morning had transformed into so many pinpricks, wetting their faces. The two men were glad to return to the warmth of the kitchen. They settled themselves at the kitchen table but Ryan still seemed uneasy.

Something had happened between his parents and Mary that was difficult for him to talk about. After a few moments of speaking to the old dog, Jasper, as a means of distraction, Ryan finally spoke, but he found it difficult to look at Oisin. Instead, he stroked the dog's head as he said quietly,

'Well. Guess someone should have told ye, Oisin. But ye know this family, all secrets and brushing things under the carpet. This is what happened as far as I could make out. Seems like Mary went for Mammy with the kitchen knife;

stabbed her in the shoulder. She would have killed her but for my Da. It was touch and go for Mammy. A few inches below and the knife would have entered her heart. Something's are hard to talk about and neither Mammy nor Da wanted to admit to anyone what really happened or why. Afterwards, Mary denied all knowledge of the attack. The only good thing to come out of it meant that the medical and the Garda know about it now and since then, Mary's been sedated a lot; in and out of the hospital here in Ballybeg. As I said, we all thought it was the best solution to have her here close to us. Family's family after all. It's not been easy but there ye have it.'

Oisin was silent. In his mind's eye, he was a young man again and his sister, Mary was there, hanging over the fence at An Teach Ban, begging him to take her away from Ballybeg and all that was there. He thought at that moment if he could just keep that memory in his mind, it would be alright. Mary could be his kid sister again.

****

That evening Oisin wrote a long email to his wife, Claire back in Kilgoolga.

He missed her more than words could say. He wrote about meeting Ryan, and what an inspirational man his nephew was, and what wonders Ryan had done to Old Mother Fahy's place. He was yet to meet Ryan's partner, Alice, a doctor, but he was looking forward to that. He had decided to move into one of Ryan's cabins for a short time to give Declan and Joyce a break. He wrote of his mother. He didn't mention Mary. It seemed that particular cloak of darkness had descended over him as well, and some things were best not spoken about.

CHAPTER FOUR

Mary did see Oisin and Ryan through the window of the cabin. She thought they were plotting something, for she decided that Ryan seemed quite agitated, and that Oisin nodded his head, as if her brother was agreeing to whatever was being said by her nephew. Mary convinced herself in those few short seconds that the two of them were deciding to move her out of the cabin, and that she would be homeless again. She felt the panic surge rise in her body. The panic always started in her stomach and moved upwards towards her throat and a few moments later, she would gasp for air, cough, and at times she had passed out. She moved away from the window so the two men couldn't see her, and flopped down on the fake yellow leather armchair in front of the television. She had the feeling that her limbs could no longer support her. Her mind could not cope with the sick feeling rising within her. Desperate thoughts flooded into her muddled mind, and in this anxious state, these thoughts were all about being homeless and alone, abandoned by those people she had trusted to save her. At different times in her life, she had twisted the panic into anger and lashed out at her perceived attackers. At other times, she had turned the anger on to herself; these were the worst times for she still had the scars. This time was different. She began to tremble, and then the tears came.

The first time Mary had felt the overwhelming panic overcome her was when she was living in Dublin. She was sixteen years of age and had left Ballybeg with the optimism and determination of youth. It had annoyed her more than she cared to admit when Oisin had left Ballybeg without her, for brother and sister had been close then, or so she thought. But then you never knew with Oisin. He had been her hero, closer in age to her than Declan and Frankie. She would have liked to have gone with her brother to Edinburgh to meet the Luchettas, who all seemed rather romantic and altogether different from the boring folk of Ballybeg. But Oisin was full of himself and anxious to spread his wings too. He had never fitted into the mould that was expected of him in Ballybeg. So he had gone off on the train and she hadn't seen or heard from him in years. It was Oisin, though, who she decided had caused her first panic attack in Dublin, for hadn't he written a letter to their mother with news that he was leaving Edinburgh and the Luchettas and heading off to Australia? Mary had wanted to go to Australia as well. If she had been able to contact him then, she would have asked him but he would have no doubt said she couldn't go with him, just like the first time.

She remembered how betrayed she had felt then. Oisin had always let her down, she decided. Always. Now he was back and getting all the attention from Declan and Frankie, and it looked like Ryan as well. If he decided to stay on no doubt Ryan would find some excuse to evict her from her present home to make room for Oisin. She was scared. Her future, which had held so much promise when she was sixteen had become an empty void of loneliness, and it was her brother, Oisin, who was to blame for her wasted life.

The panic attack lasted for just a few minutes and then she took a deep breath. The fear passed from her as quickly as it had come on, and Oisin and Ryan were nowhere to be seen. She went into the small kitchen and boiled the electric kettle to make herself a cup of coffee. Then she stirred three teaspoons of white sugar into the cup. Sugar helped her at times like this. The sweet taste of coffee and sugar relaxed her and somehow the panic disappeared from her mind, if only for a short time. She curled up on the armchair and shut her eyes. A few moments later, she fell asleep.

****

Oisin moved in to one of Ryan's cabins a few days later. Although Declan and Joyce had welcomed him, it was good to have his own space again, if just for a few weeks. The cabin was in need of repair so he set about doing some of the carpentry work that was needed. It felt good to hold a hammer and chisel again. He had retired from his carpentry business in Kilgoolga a few years ago, but he still enjoyed the feel of wood and the joy of making things again, even if it was just replacing or repairing boards that had come adrift. It was early March and work had to be done to get the cabins ready for the guests who would be arriving in April. Ryan told him that all the cabins were fully booked for the summer, and that included the one he now lived in.

'I'll be gone by then,' Oisin assured him with a cheeky grin.

'Ye can always stay with Alice and me.' Ryan had developed quite a liking for his wandering uncle.

Oisin thanked him but he knew in his heart that he would have left Ballybeg by then. He visited his mother every day and every day he sat by her bedside. It was the waiting that was hard. The waiting for the end of a life and no plans could be made until that day arrived. Oisin knew it would be just a matter of weeks now for Annie, but when? He was glad of the distraction of helping Ryan.

Days went by and there was no sign of Mary. He

wondered if she was aware that he had moved in to one of the cabins, or whether she even cared. His cabin was perched by itself on the slope of the hill and not close to hers but she must have seen him wandering past. Every morning he liked to go down to the beach whatever the weather, and to walk along the sand, to pause and sit on a rock, and watch the waves. All the memories were there but as the days went past, it all became more familiar and the memories lessened. Surely Mary must have seen him pass by in the morning, or in the evening when he sometimes joined Alice and Ryan for a meal or a cosy chat. No mention was made of Mary in these chats. It was as if everything about her that could be, had been said.

One late afternoon, after he had been there a week, he made up his mind to visit Mary. He really didn't know what he should say to her but it was his brotherly duty, he assured himself. After all, he planned to leave as soon as his mother was put to rest and the funeral was over. Then everyone could resume their lives again. He had things he wanted to do before he left for Kilgoolga and home to Claire. It was with some trepidation that he knocked on the door of his sister's cabin. Given all that had been said about her and what he had experienced, he wasn't sure if he would be welcomed or not. Perhaps she might stab him with her umbrella point again, or worse?

Mary opened the door just a little so that Oisin only saw her face and the mop of curly grey hair.

'What do you want?'

'To talk. Can I come in?'

'What do you want to talk about?'

'Well, let me in, Mary and ye will find out, sure enough.'

'I don't like people in the cabin.'

'Let me in, Mary. It's perishin' out here.'

It had started to rain and the air was cold. Oisin, despite his heavy coat, shivered. He still hadn't acclimatised himself to the Irish weather. Forty years in outback Australia had softened him. He could bear the heat now, not the cold.

His words must have made an impression for Mary opened the door. He entered the small front living room, the exact replica of the cabin that he stayed in.

There was the same décor but the room was untidy for it looked as if Mary had just emerged from her bed. She hadn't combed her hair nor had she removed the heavy black mascara or eye shadow. Black lines ran down her cheeks. Mary was theatrical and had a penchant for heavy eye makeup which often surprised people when they met her. The dressing gown that she appeared to have just flung on when she heard the knock on the door clung rather shabbily around her thin body, and when she reached for the inevitable cigarette, the gown slipped from her shoulder exposing part of her breast. This wasn't the Mary who Oisin remembered as his kid sister. In fact, his nervousness increased as he stood there, given what had happened on the beach, and what Ryan had told him about Mary's mental state. His usual quick wit and optimism failed him for the woman in front of him appeared a stranger. Mary lit a cigarette, her hand trembled slightly, and then she blew the smoke in Oisin's direction. He coughed slightly.

'Did Ryan send you?'

'No. I just wanted to see you. We haven't had a chance to talk much.'

Mary laughed.

'There's nothing we have to say to each other.' Angry, she swept a tartan travelling rug and a few magazines onto the floor from one of the yellow leather armchairs. Then she sat down and lit another cigarette. Oisin decided to sit down as well so he perched on the other chair. Now brother and sister faced each other across a coffee table piled high with an assortment of magazines, books and leftover food. An awkward silence followed.

'I don't really like you much, Oisin.'

This was a surprise.

'Well, we haven't seen each other for a long

time,' Oisin said after a few moments. 'And ye never kept in touch.'

'Nor did you. Just took off to Edinburgh and the wild blue yonder. I could have been dead for all ye cared.'

'I thought ye had made quite a name for yeself in the art world. That's what I was led to believe.'

'Little do you know.'

Another uneasy silence followed broken only by the lashing of the rain on the window pane. The weather had been miserable for days. Oisin wondered if he should leave but his curiosity was aroused in a rather unexpected way. After all, the version that he had heard from his mother in letters to him was that Mary had become a rather famous artist in London although his mother had fretted that Mary never visited.

'Mammy said ye were famous. Very proud of ye, she was.'

Mary appeared to find the notion of her mother's pride somewhat amusing for she laughed.

'My mother was always a fantasist.'

This wasn't the Annie that Oisin knew but he said nothing.

'What has happened to ye, Mary?' He asked in his quiet voice, fearing another outburst.

'Life happened.'

'Well... ?'

'Just that. You'd better go.'

Oisin felt slightly peeved at the tone of dismissal in his sister's voice. It was a bit like being told off by an authoritarian school master. He stood up.

'I'll go then,' he said. He put on his tweed cap and coat. Mary didn't look up.

As he opened the door of the cabin, she called out,

'Ryan wants me to leave, ye know,' she said. 'I've nowhere else to go but no one cares.'

Oisin didn't hear. He was already outside. Horizontal rain greeted him, and he just wanted some peace.

****

The next few days Oisin spent helping Ryan getting the cabins ready for the season. They worked well together and neither man mentioned Mary. In fact, Mary was nowhere to be seen. When they passed by her cabin, all was quiet with no sign of life. For the ever optimistic Oisin, his sister's behaviour was odd, bordering on the extreme. He decided it would be best to leave her alone for a bit before approaching her again.

His days became a routine of an early morning walk along the shore, helping Ryan until lunchtime and walking into Ballybeg to sit beside his mother.

Then, back to have a quick chat to Joyce and Declan before spending the night in the cabin, a place that was becoming more familiar to him as the days went by. Once a week he called Claire on a video link so as to keep his wife in the picture and he wrote her an email every second day or so. Life takes on routine in an altogether rapid way, he thought as he pressed the send button to Claire. His wife was managing fine without him. He wondered how long he should stay away. This waiting at his mother's hospital bed was a difficult thing. Sometimes, Annie wanted to talk. Other times she slept. When she was sleeping, he would sit quietly and study her face, and think about her. She looked peaceful, sleeping with an occasional snore. Sometimes, she woke, and when she saw who was beside her bed, she smiled and reached out her hand so they could hold each other. Then Oisin knew that his mother did love him. That made all the difference.

One day he saw Mary again. He had visited his mother in the morning and in the afternoon he decided to keep to his familiar routine and to walk a mile or so along the beach. It was one of those magical days in the West of Ireland when everything seemed perfect and, conscious of that perfection in nature, Oisin felt a wonderful sense of wellbeing as he strode along the sandy beach on this bucolic March afternoon. Life felt good. The sadness of seeing Annie that morning, slowly sinking away, was replaced in his mind with a peaceful feeling for Annie, too, was at peace, he reasoned. It was just a matter of days now for his mother, the doctor told him. Coming to terms with the reality of having to say goodbye to his mother was difficult for him. The daily walk along the beach had become solace for his soul.

Whispers of clouds in the blue sky and a slight breeze made for a pleasant spring day. The snowbells peeped up from the once frozen ground. All was quiet except for a flock of rowdy seagulls screeching and circling above his head, swooping downwards towards the shoreline, then as one lifting upwards as if all were joined by a thread. The birds, too, seemed to be enjoying the better weather. Then he saw Mary.

When she noticed him, she cried out,

'Oisin. Oisin.'

He hesitated. The previous meeting between brother and sister had been tense but it appeared that she obviously wanted to see him, for she kept calling his name. By the time she caught up with him she was so out of breath that she had to bend over and breathe deeply before she spoke.

'Oisin. Ryan says I can stay, isn't that wonderful news?'

This announcement was a puzzle for Oisin for

he had assumed that Ryan had been resigned to his Aunt Mary living in the cabin, even if it had meant that there was one less cabin to rent out for the season. He said nothing.

This was a different Mary than the one he had met the other day. She had obviously taken time to dress herself this time. An expensive looking powder blue winter coat with large brown buttons, a stylish woollen scarf and a matching blue and brown tartan cap covered her grey curly hair. Mary could have been dressed for a night out at a swanky city restaurant. Even her makeup had been applied with care. Bright red lipstick, eye liner and mascara, this was a new Mary.

'I've decided to throw a party to celebrate the good news,' she said. 'I've invited Declan and Joyce, even Mairead, and Ryan and Alice of course. A family affair. You must come.'

Then she hooked her arm in his and the two of them walked further along the beach scattering the seagulls that had taken up residence for a few moments on the sand.

'When is this taking place?' asked Oisin after a few moments.

'Oh, sometime soon,' was the reply and Mary laughed. A few seconds later, she stopped and faced Oisin.

'I never will be homeless again, Oisin, will I?'

'What do you mean, homeless? Have ye been without a home before?'

'Aye. Many's the time.'

'How could that be? Ye had everything going for ye, didn't ye? How could ye end up homeless, Mary?'

Mary unhooked her arm from his and kicked the sand with her leather boot.

'Well, I just did. Oisin. Can we leave it at that.'

Oisin decided that perhaps that was the best course of action in the circumstances. He nodded.

'Well, Mary. I'd love to join ye in yer cabin for a party.'

Hearing his words, Mary hugged him and planted a lavish red kiss onto his cheek.

'Ye always was my favourite brother,' she whispered into his good ear.

CHAPTER FIVE

There came a day like no other. Everything was calm that April morning. Oisin woke to blue skies and just the gentlest of breezes. After a light breakfast of tea and toast, he headed to the beach. He had been back in Ballybeg a month and it felt as if he had never left. The town had changed its image and shaken off the old certainties of the past but the rocks and the sand beneath his feet were timeless. There was solid comfort in knowing that whatever the human population did to try to alter the landscape, nature would prevail in the end.

As he strolled without much purpose in mind, just enjoying being alive on such a near perfect morning, his thoughts turned, as they inevitably did these days to his mother, Annie, lying in her hospital bed, while time slipped gently from her. He wondered if she was awake this morning and could see such a blue sky from her bed. He hoped that she could. He knew that she had grown to love the world around Ballybeg with its constant changing weather and its motley crowd of inhabitants. Eighteen-years-old Annie had a made a home for herself in this place so far from the London she had known. Lately, however, when he sat beside her bed and when she was able to speak, her talk was of the London she knew, of Camden and people from her past. She talked about her mother and father as if they were beside her. And when she spoke of her father, dead in Hitler's war, and of her beloved brother dying on a foreign shore in that same dreadful war, Annie was back there in time, reliving it all, and her eyes shone with a vibrancy he had never seen before.

'You wouldn't remember Uncle George, would you, Oisin? Your grandmother's brother,' she said to him one day. 'He and Mum came over to Ballybeg once and he made quite an impression on Ma Murphy, remember Ma Murphy, Oisin, you must remember Ma, Oisin.'

Oisin did, indeed remember Ma and Pa Murphy from the pub. His father played the fiddle there and his Uncle Mick got drunk.

'Aye, I remember Uncle George. Had quite an eye for the lassies.'

Annie laughed. It was good to hear her laugh again. When she laughed, everyone always joined in for Annie's laugh was infectious. This time the laughter brought on a fit of coughing. Oisin held her hand.

'All those memories, Ma,' he said after a few moments had passed.

An image came into his mind of that childhood adventure with his mother holding their hands, for Mary came too. London, crowded and noisy, not at all like the peace of Ballybeg. Mary and he were just children then. It all seemed frightening and yet, exciting too, for his mother had been different there, freer somehow but he never could understand why. The three of them had travelled by train and then boarded the ferry across the Irish Sea to his dying grandmother, and the funeral after. Sitting beside his mother in her hospital bed was one of those same moments, he decided and he felt sad. He wanted to say something to Annie then; tell her that he remembered; that he would be there for her, just the way she had been for her own mother. But she closed her eyes and few minutes later, he heard her breathing deeper and she had fallen asleep.

The English nurse from London bustled in a few moments later, and when she saw that Annie was sleeping, she said,

'Best leave her now, Oisin. She looks so peaceful, doesn't she? Not a care in the world.'

She gently pulled the cover around Annie's shoulders and smiled.

'She's a grand old lady, your mother.'

'Aye, that she is.'

That was the day he wondered did he know his mother at all? The only thing they had between them were the memories of his childhood, and his going away. He hadn't seen Annie for forty years.

They had written brief letters over the years but the communication between them was an altogether spasmodic sort of thing. Annie was a poor letter writer at the best of times. Oisin's own life was one of drama and upheaval. There had been no need to worry his mother, and if she had known, what could she have done? So he decided best keep it that way. Now, when he sat by her bedside, he wondered if he should have done more to keep in touch with her but regrets are things best forgotten. There was no way the past could be changed. He had made his decision to make his home at the other end of the earth, and that was that. Those forty years of Annie's life would remain something he knew nothing about.

He strolled towards the shoreline and looked across the sea but his thoughts were still with his mother and her life. Had it broken her Catholic heart that she had loved two men? It wasn't such a sin now, he decided. In a way, he was glad that she had found happiness with his Uncle Mick, if only for a short time. After Mick died, what did she do? He heard that Silvio Luchetta had paid her a visit but this was after Oisin had left for Australia. It was unlikely that the wealthy Italian and his mother would have been lovers but she was still young then. He decided it was one of those secrets that would never be known and he doubted if his mother would remember anyhow. There was no need to press her on this rather delicate subject, especially now when she was at the end. His own life had not been without temptation, so who was he to judge?

Sometimes Declan came with him to sit by their mother, other times it was just himself. Declan was a good companion but his world and the world of Oisin were poles apart. There was a familial bond between the brothers but it was a questionable one. Declan's life was Ballybeg. That was the difference between them.

It was a pensive man who walked back along the shoreline. His morning plan was to finish the work on the last cabin, and then in the afternoon walk into Ballybeg to sit beside his mother's bedside once again, and wait.

****

Oisin was surprised when he entered the hospital because his mother wasn't in her usual place in the ward she shared with three other elderly women. The English nurse told him that Annie had been moved to a room of her own. When he enquired as to why that had happened, the nurse just said that they needed her bed for another patient. It didn't seem all that plausible to Oisin but he said nothing, just followed the nurse along the corridor to a small private room. He was even more surprised when he saw Annie because she was sitting up in a chair beside her bed, the blue hospital cover around her thin shoulders. Her eyes were shut. The nurse shook her shoulder gently and the cover slipped slightly to reveal her almost skeletal frame. She looked so frail and fragile not at all like the mother he remembered from his childhood.

'Here's Oisin to see you, Annie.'

Still Annie did not stir and the nurse had to shake her harder.

'She wanted to sit in her chair this morning. Not lie in bed. It's what she wanted and we thought we would let her be. She's slipping away, Oisin,' said the nurse.

There were tears behind her eyes. She had grown very fond of Annie and it was good to talk about the places they both knew in London. The nurse had an uncle and aunt who lived in Camden, not far from where Annie grew up, it was a connection. The nurse used to visit her cousins and they all would take the tube into town, to wander along Oxford Street and look at the shops. When they talked about London, the nurse said, it was as if Annie had never left. It was a strange thing but then, you never know what another person is thinking, do you? Especially one who had lived such a long life like Annie.

'Your mother and I both like living in Ireland, you know. Well, I married an Irishman like Annie, and home is home wherever you are, but sometimes it's good to talk to someone who knows a bit about your world, isn't it now?'

'Aye, that it is. I'm glad ye have been here for her. I never was.'

'Now, don't you fret, Oisin. You're here now, aren't you? And that means so much to your mother. She told me she was so proud of you and all you had achieved. Just like Mick said you would. Who was Mick?'

'My uncle. Dad's brother. He lived with us at An Teach Ban.'

'Ah,' said the nurse.

Whether she heard Mick's name or not, but at that point, Annie opened her eyes.

'Is that you, Mick?'

'No, Mammy. It's me... Oisin.'

He perched on the side of the bed and gently held her left hand. This hand was wrinkled with age and the two rings on her finger were loose. The two rings she always wore, her wedding ring and Mick's ring.

'Ah,' Annie said. 'I thought you were Mick come for me.'

'Not yet, Mammy. He's waiting for ye.' He smiled.

They sat like that for a few minutes. It was comforting to be beside her, holding her hand. *This is the mother I love*, he thought.

'I'd better go now,' he said after a few more minutes. 'Let ye have some rest.

Annie smiled. 'I've plenty of time for rest now, son,' she said.

'Aye that ye have.'

As he stood up to leave, she placed her withered old hand onto his arm and looked into his eyes.

'I did my best for all of you, didn't I?'

'Of course ye did, Ma. I'm sorry I wasn't here for ye more.'

'You're here now, Oisin.'

'Aye, that I am.'

'Makes all the difference, you know,' Annie coughed. 'You being here. All my boys together. Where's Frankie?'

'He's in Dublin but he plans to see ye next weekend.'

'That's good. You know, when he left the priesthood I was sad but now I'm happy to see him with Ellen. They're happy.'

'Like two lovebirds, Ma.'

'Old lovebirds.' Annie chuckled which brought on another spell of coughing.

She sank back into the chair and closed her eyes.

'I'll be off now, Ma,' Oisin said and he kissed her on the cheek.

Annie opened her eyes and took hold of his arm again.

'You know, Oisin... Mary's a bad girl,' she whispered and then she closed her eyes once again.

****

Mary sat by the window of the cabin and stared at the large, black, artist's portfolio case that she had brought with her from London. Once, in a fit of rage, she had burnt fifty of her paintings. She had taken the unframed paintings and made a fire in the back garden of Anton's house. At the time this was a magnificent release. She remembered the day well. It had been a perfect sunny day and there wasn't a cloud in the sky but Anton had told her that she had to stay indoors, and paint. How furious she had been with him then, so as an act of revenge, she had decided to destroy her paintings, the ones she considered her worst. When she threw them, one by one, onto the fire, she laughed out aloud. She painted when the black moods were upon her, and Anton was nowhere to be seen that fateful day so he wouldn't know any of this. There would be an argument when he discovered the missing ones but she didn't care. Anton could only think of money, not the creative talent that he had nurtured in her, or so he always reminded her when they argued. So she had kept about thirty of her best paintings from the flames as a way of reminding herself of what she had been capable of then. That was another life, Anton was another life, and her art was another life.

The paintings she saved lay hidden within the black case. She knew these were her best work. She had been inspired when she worked on them. It was perverse perhaps, but she hadn't wanted to see them destroyed; so the lucky thirty had remained out of sight in that black case for years. She refused to open the case. It was like a genie in a bottle. If she opened the case, all her past life would come back to her in a kind of painful rush, a reminder of Anton and what she had been then.

The case, covered in dust, seemed to be mocking her. But she decided she had to open it because she remembered she had packed a stack of embossed invitation cards within it, neatly hidden in a large white envelope. She remembered a sketchbook was there as well with nude pencil drawings of Anton and charcoal ones of him as well. She sketched him one day when he was wearing his brown suede Gucci jacket with a red silk cravat around his neck and that arrogant look on his face. They had an argument when he saw her drawing. He said that it didn't look like him at all but she knew she had captured the real Anton. She kept that sketch.

This had all come about because of her somewhat impetuous invitation to Oisin about a party. She and Anton used to host fabulous parties in London. Invitations would be sent out and the great and the good of the art world came along. She thought it would be a wonderful thing to do again, send out special invitations, just like she used to do. But Ballybeg wasn't London and she would only be able to invite a few of the family. She had no friends in Ballybeg. People she knew had either moved away or died and the ones, who stayed, probably didn't much want to know her. No doubt word had got round about her behaviour. She didn't care what people thought anyway. She rarely moved from her cabin and to all intents and purpose, lived a hermit's life. Only the few family members looked out for her. Perhaps invitations would not be needed for such a small number. Maybe, the portfolio case need not be opened after all?

Mary carried the case, unopened, and tucked it behind her tattered and battered old leather suitcase. The suitcase that had been her travelling companion for years but now, like herself, showing the signs of an item which was no longer of service. She sighed. The portfolio case could remain there behind her old suitcase for now, out of sight and out of mind. She had no wish to let that particular genie out at the moment, if ever.

She heard honking outside the cabin door and when she peered through the curtain she saw Oisin, walking with his head down, deep in thought with Ryan's six pet geese following him, one behind each other and in a perfect straight line like soldiers on parade. Oisin paused for a moment and looked towards Mary's cabin as if he was thinking about coming in. She hid her face from him and when she looked through the window a few minutes later, he was no longer there. He must have quickened his pace because the six geese, their wings flapping and all of them honking much louder had sped up and were intent on catching him. Mary disliked the geese and avoided them as much as she could. Oisin always had a way with animals, she thought.

****

That evening when Oisin was preparing to go to bed his cell phone rang. It was the hospital. When he answered the call, he heard the unmistakable accent of the English nurse from London.

'Your mother's failing fast, Oisin.' She said in her soft voice.

There was silence from Oisin while he tried to come to terms with her words. A few seconds later and then he spoke,

'Are the others there? My brother, Declan? Ryan? Mairead?'

'We're calling them now.'

'Thank you,' he said. 'I'll see Ryan. We'll drive in. I don't fancy walking tonight into Ballybeg. It's blowing an almighty gale out there.'

'I think that's wise, Oisin.'

He wondered had the hospital let Mary know? They were mother and daughter after all, even if they didn't see eye to eye.

'Has anyone contacted Mary? My sister...'

'Mary?'

'Aye. Mary.'

'I didn't know Annie had a daughter.'

This was a revelation. His mother would surely have mentioned Mary. Had Mary visited her mother in the hospital but told no one of their relationship? Or perhaps, in Mary's mental state, she hadn't bothered to visit at all. It was strange. After all, Mary had moved back to Ballybeg and Oisin had assumed that it was because Annie was dying. Maybe there was another reason Mary was here?

'My sister lives in one of Ryan's cabins here in Ballybeg. I thought she would have been to see our mother.'

'No, Oisin... unless one of the other nurses

might have met her. Seamus O'Maera was looking after Annie before I came on the scene but Seamus retired a few months ago and I took over from him. No one said anything to me about a daughter but then, I've only been working here about three months.'

There was silence on the line and then the nurse spoke,

'You have another brother, Oisin, don't you?'

'Aye. Frankie. He lives in Dublin.'

A few seconds later, the nurse spoke again,

'I've met Frankie,' she said. 'I have his number. I'll call him.'

'Thank you. Will he be able to get here before?'

'I hope so, Oisin. I do hope so.'

It took Oisin a few moments to fully realize what was happening. Of course, he knew it was inevitable, that his mother was dying... that's why he had come back to Ballybeg from Australia, but understanding it on an intellectual level was an altogether different matter than accepting it on an emotional one. Annie had always been there for them all and logic dictated this fact, but sometimes logic is a poor bedfellow to the emotions.

He dressed quickly and pulled on a woolly hat, gloves and a winter coat. It was cold outside and he would need all the warm clothes to keep out the chill. There was a light on in Mary's cabin. He knocked on the door.

'It's me, Mary... Oisin.'

'What do you want?'

'Open the door, Mary. It's important.'

'Go away. I'm busy.'

'Mary, please. It's Mammy.'

'It's late.'

'I know, Mary but I think ye should come.'

It seemed like an eternity before the pale face of Mary opened the door, just wide enough that Oisin could see her face and her hand.

'What's happened?' she asked.

'The hospital just rang me. Mammy mightn't last the night. They're ringing everyone. They've let Frankie know. I'm off to see Ryan now to take us in to Ballybeg.'

'I won't come.'

'Why, Mary? In the name of God, she's your mother.'

'You can say goodbye to her then, for me.'

The door closed. Oisin was left standing there in the cold with the rain dampening his face and a jumble of thoughts jostling around in his mind.

****

They were all together, waiting. The English nurse and his brother, Declan, Joyce and their daughter,

Mairead, all four of them looking forlorn. At first glance, Oisin thought that he had been too late, that Annie had already passed and his brother had been the last one to see her, to say goodbye.

Ryan had driven fast into Ballybeg. Not a word was spoken about Mary. She seemed to have been erased from the drama so Oisin said nothing. Alice came with them and when she saw everyone looking upset, she had a word to the English nurse.

'Dr Diallo is on duty tonight,' she said to Ryan. 'I'll see what's happened.'

After, what seemed an age, Alice returned with Dr Diallo by her side. Dr Diallo was from Senegal. Everyone called him Dr Di. He was tall and thin with black eyes, fine boned hands and manicured nails. He had fled from Senegal, and Ireland had given him refuge. For that, he was eternally grateful. Everyone liked Dr Di.

He spoke English with a French accent and the nurses considered him handsome.

'Thank you for coming,' he said, 'I am sad that it is such a difficult time for you all but please to know that Madame Kelly is at peace. We 'ave made Madame a comfortable bed to sleep in, and the priest, he is with her now.'

'Can we see her, Doctor?' asked Mairead as tears welled up behind her eyes. One valiant tear escaped and rolled down her cheek.

'I think after the priest has seen her, you will be able to, but please, she is very weak. I would advise if you do not all be with her together. Just one or two should be with Madame, please.' He spread his hands in a Gallic gesture. 'She is at peace and should not be troubled.'

Dr Di had seen much of death but it was never easy. Annie had reached that thin veil between life and death, and Death was beckoning her.

Dr Di whispered something to Alice and then the English nurse joined them. Alice nodded her head. No one could make out what they were saying. When Alice returned to stand beside Ryan, she looked thoughtful.

'Dr Di is right,' she said. 'Too many people crowding into Annie's room at this stage might cause her some distress. She is barely conscious now. Prepare yourselves, she may not recognize anyone.'

No one spoke. What was unfolding before their eyes was difficult to imagine, and painful to experience.

As Alice said those words, the priest appeared. He carefully closed the door to Annie's room, coughed and shook his head. The priest was an old man and had been Annie's priest for over twenty years, ever since Fr Byrne retired. Holding his stick for support and bent almost double, he gave the impression that he had administered too many last rites, this last one an altogether difficult one. Annie was a good Catholic woman; she would be missed by all. He felt sympathy for the family, all huddled together, knowing that this would be the last time any of them would see a beloved family member. The priest wiped his watery blue eyes with a clean white handkerchief, coughed again and then said,

'A sad day indeed. Mrs Kelly is quite prepared, I want ye all to know. A brave wee woman, indeed.' And with that, he shuffled off, still coughing.

Declan and Joyce went into Annie's room first, followed by Ryan and Mairead. No one said anything. Mairead was crying when she and Ryan came out of the room, and her mother put an arm around her shoulders. Mairead sobbed in Joyce's arms, like a baby. It was quite distressing to witness. Ryan looked sad. Declan, the faithful brother who had looked after Annie till the last, appeared to be in a state of bewilderment. He sat down on one of the uncomfortable hospital chairs and put his head in his hands.

Then it was Oisin's turn. When he saw his mother his first thought was that she had already passed away for she looked so peaceful, lying on her back with one hand resting next to her heart. He touched her arm, ever so gently, but he heard no breath. Thinking that it was because of the deafness in his left ear, he tried again. This time his fingers explored her neck for the throbbing of the artery. A very faint pulse was his reward and he sat down on the chair beside her bed. He studied the pale face of his mother almost as if he was capturing the image and storing it into his subconscious for later, to remember. He watched her for a few minutes longer and then he shook her arm again, stronger this time, and said,

'Are ye awake, Mammy?'

Trite words, indeed, for he didn't expect an answer. But Annie did hear for she opened both her eyes and, seeing the shadow of a man beside her, whispered,

'Is that you, Frankie?'

What a moment that was for Oisin. Consumed with grief, and something of remorse for his long absence away, to hear his mother asking for his elder brother was a bitter pill. Even at the end of her life she was asking for Frankie. It had always been Frankie.

'No', he replied. 'It's Oisin.'

A very faint smile arrived on Annie's lips. She reached out and with one hand, weak now; she placed this hand onto his arm.

'Ah, my hero. My Oisin.'

Then she closed her eyes again.

****

He got the call on his cell phone at precisely a quarter to four in the morning. The phone woke him for he had fallen into a deep sleep.

'I'm sorry, Oisin,' he heard the unmistakable voice of the English nurse. 'Your mother passed away at three thirty. She went ever so gently. I think you were the last person from the family to see her.'

Still full of sleep and not quite awake, Oisin murmured,

'Did my brother... Frankie... did he get there in time? He was driving from Dublin that night...'

'No, Oisin. Frankie wasn't there.'

'Ah.'

Oisin sank back into his bed. Sleep would not return to him that night.

****

It was a quiet day when Annie Kelly was laid to rest. When Oisin walked into the Church of St Peter and St Paul, he was uneasy, for this was not a place of sanctuary for him, rather the opposite, for it was here that he had not known any peace there. His old teacher, Baldy Lawrence had mocked him beneath its sanctified walls. Fr O'Malley, the severe and unforgiving priest of his boyhood, taunted him on those occasions he was unable to escape if he had happened to be in the wrong place at the wrong time. Many the time, Fr O'Malley seized upon him in the church, and all manner of tirades would spew forth from the priest's mouth. According to Fr O'Malley, Oisin was an evil lad, destined to fail, just cast in the same unfortunate mould as his obstinate uncle, Mick for the priest had never forgave Mick for his rebellion against the church and all its teachings.

Then there was brother, Frankie, an altar boy, the apple of his mother's eye and a worthwhile recruit to the priesthood, according to both Baldy and Fr O'Malley. The memories weren't pleasant. He sat down in the front pew next to Declan and Frankie. Mary was nowhere to be seen. There was his mother's coffin in front of him, covered in lilies with the smell of incense wafting like a soothing balm in the air.

The old priest whom he had met at the hospital shuffled down the aisle and everyone rose. Annie's funeral began. By Ballybeg standards, this was a small funeral for Annie had outlived most of her peers so it was more or less a family affair. No one from her own family was there. Annie had long since lost all connection with the London of her youth. This was a Ballybeg event. Prayers were said and Oisin bowed his head. Then the old priest told them what a faithful servant Annie had been to the church and how she would be missed by all but now she was safe in the arms of Jesus.

Then it was Frankie's turn. Standing in front of the congregation, his years in the priesthood were evident to all for he was a powerful speaker and knew how to engage an audience. His mother was a shining light and it was she who kept the family together. He spoke of the memories he had of his mother and joked about her sometimes English ways. A sad occasion, he said, but his mother had lived a good life and was a faithful wife and a loving mother to them all. He didn't mention Mick.

As a mark of respect to his mother Oisin took communion with all the others. He bowed his head and said a silent prayer. An image of Mick and Annie came into his head at that moment, together in bed; he wondered if he would ever be able to forget or would that image taunt him to the end of his days. Then he opened his eyes. The mass ended, and he and his brothers, with Ryan, lifted Annie's coffin and carried it down the aisle. There was still no sign of Mary.

It was at the graveside that he saw Mary. She was wearing a long black dress to her ankles and a black hat with a veil around her face to cover her eyes. She stood apart from her brothers and didn't acknowledge them. Oisin thought she had been weeping but he wasn't sure because of the veil. It was when she lifted the veil and wiped her eyes that he knew that she had, indeed, wept. Somehow, he was relieved to see this. Whatever had happened between Mary and her mother at least Mary was there to say goodbye.

At a funeral we grieve for the one who has left us, but buried within our sorrow, we also become aware of our own mortality. Oisin, seeing the mother he loved laid to rest, and the sober and tearful faces around him, knew there was something he had to do before he, too, would be laid to rest. There was much to do.

It was an altogether jolly affair for Annie's wake. Family and a few friends gathered at An Teach Ban, Annie's home for a lifetime, the place where she had toiled and loved and grown old. The English nurse and Seamus O'Maera along with their partners were there and a few of Annie's old women friends. Declan proposed a toast to his mother with a whiskey for his mother did so like her tipple, and even if she had never become fond of the Guinness, a small glass of whiskey once a week had become her routine for years. Then there was all talk of Annie and much laughter.

It was sometime later in the afternoon that Mary arrived looking sombre. She had hurried away from the cemetery as soon as the service ended.

103

Now she appeared without the black hat and veil but still wearing her long black dress, black stockings and black shoes. She had not tidied herself at all nor had she made any attempt to fix her makeup. She must have been crying because the mascara had run down her cheeks making her look slightly ghoulish.

'Come on in, Mary,' said Declan when he saw her standing at the door. 'There's a drink here for ye an' plenty to eat.'

'I won't be staying,' replied Mary. 'But I'll take the drink.'

'What's that ye be havin', Mary? We've whiskey, wine, gin, orange juice an' I think there's even some vodka here...,'

'I'll take a glass of white wine, thank you.'

She seemed ill at ease as if something had happened. When she entered the room and everyone saw her, chattering ceased for a few seconds. It was quite an awkward moment for all.

Soon the talk started again. Mary sipped her glass of wine and when she was offered a tray of nibbles and sausage rolls, she shook her head.

'I don't eat,' she said.

Oisin had taken notice of what was happening. He had been enjoying a chat with Mairead's husband, Sean, a fisherman, when his sister entered the room. He wondered if he should approach Mary and offer her an olive branch. The last few encounters between them had been fraught. He was about to talk to her when she suddenly turned towards Joyce and, with a threatening gesture, she said,

'You never liked my mother.'

Joyce, caught unawares, could only mutter a denial.

'That's not true, Mary. And you know it.'

Her remark seemed to incense Mary for she threw her half-filled glass of wine onto the floor. The glass smashed into pieces.

No one spoke.

Declan, the peace maker, tried to pacify his sister but she turned on him as well and, like a cornered viper, she spat out,

'Say what you will, Declan. Your wife's a whore.'

This was too much for the gentle Declan.

'Get out,' he shouted. 'And don't ye come back into this house, until ye apologize to my wife.'

Instead of being intimidated by his remark, Mary laughed.

'Don't worry,' she said. 'I know when I'm not welcome.'

And she flounced out of the room leaving behind a shocked silence. Annie's wake had turned into an altogether different affair.

****

For the next few days Oisin avoided Mary. He had been astonished by her behaviour towards Joyce but when he approached Declan and tried to engage him in conversation about the event, his brother wouldn't be drawn leaving Oisin puzzled about this particular family dynamic. Declan muttered something about it being a fairly common occurrence between the two women. It usually resolved itself after a few days when Mary arrived at their door as if nothing had happened.

Oisin decided then and there that he had been so long apart from his brother and Mary, and indeed life in Ballybeg, that it was time for him to leave. Life had moved on for them all, and with his mother's passing, there really wasn't any reason for him to stay much longer. Ireland would always be his place of birth and it was here that he had spent his formative years but his home was in a different place on the planet in faraway Kilgoolga with his Aussie wife, Claire. He looked around the small cabin which had been his home for two months and heard the soft patter of the rain on the window pane. It was one of those early mornings in the west of Ireland when the mist came down over the sea and brought with it gentle raindrops. It was an altogether nostalgic moment for this Irishman. He had come home for the memories but that's all they were now, just memories. His family, although welcoming, had been through forty years of life here and his world held different experiences, none of which they knew anything about as he knew nothing about theirs. It was time to leave.

He spent the next few days absorbing as much as he could about Ballybeg. He spent hours walking along the beach as if to capture all those memories and draw them into his mind so that he could recall them later on when he was back with Claire and so far from the sea. He loved to perch on the rocks and watch the waves breaking on the shoreline. In this solitude, he found peace of sorts.

It was now five days since he had last seen Mary at his mother's wake. He said his goodbyes to the few friends he knew in Ballybeg, Seamus O'Meara and the English nurse among others. He knew he would never see any of them again. When no one was about he thanked his nephew, Ryan for his hospitality and wished him well in his endeavours with the organic garden and the cabins. Declan and Joyce arranged a farewell dinner at An Teach Ban for him and all the family were there, except Frankie and his wife, Ellen. Oisin had been invited to stay the night in Dublin with the two of them before his departure from Ireland. He was glad Frankie and he were friends at last. Frankie had changed since he left the priesthood. Marriage suited him.

It was another evening of memories for them all. Oisin wondered if they had invited Mary for there was no sign of her. Her cabin door was locked and the curtains were drawn every time he passed by.

'Have ye seen anything of Mary these past few days?' he asked Declan when they managed some peace away from the chattering and the laughter.

'Mary keeps to herself these days. She has her dark days and then there's a change, she's a different person then. Trouble is, none of us know when the old Mary will reappear,' Declan added with a sigh.

'It's hard seein' her like this.'

'Aye. Sure it is. She's not the Mary of our childhood, is she now?'

'No, ye are right enough there. Us lads used to tease her a lot, didn't we now? But she always got her way in the end.'

'Spoilt. She was the apple of Da's eyes, remember?' Declan looked thoughtful.

'Aye. And Mick spoilt her too.'

'Funny how we all turn out.' Declan added. 'Look at ye. Always thought ye were meant for bigger things.'

Oisin laughed. 'Don't know about that,' he replied with a grin. 'Just knew I had to spread me wings, sort of thing. Left ye to do it all. I should have made more of an effort.'

'Don't beat yerself up about it. What was meant to be was meant to be. We none of us know what's it all about or what's ahead of us, for that matter. All we have is the moment so let's enjoy it, what do ye say?'

Declan poured them both another whiskey. Oisin's head had begun to spin. He put his arm around Declan's shoulders.

'That's very phi-los-ophical of ye, brother o' mine. When did ye become all phi-los-ophical?' He had difficulty pronouncing 'philosophical' and the word came out rather slurred.

'Been thinkin' of all these things these days. Must be getting older an' wondering if there's anything beyond all this.' Declan waved his hand in the air as if to receive an answer from beyond.

'Aye. Don't think any of us knows this, old man.'

'Ye are right there, Oisin but ye might be closer to knowin' than any of us, ye being a thinker, that is. Me, I'm just a poor farmer makin' do.'

'Looks like ye are makin' do quite well by the look of it.'

'Aye. Got me Joycie to thank for this. She's one in a million, that woman. Let's drink a toast to the women.'

The two brothers clunked their glasses, drank

and then Declan said,

'Is yer Claire one in a million too?'

'Aye, Declan. Sure she is. A real Aussie battler is my Claire. Calls a spade a spade, not a fork.' He giggled.

'Doubt if I'll ever be meetin' yer missus... don't like the thought o' fly... flyin all that way in a tin box with wings.' Declan was beginning to slur his words as well and the two brothers had to prop each other up, an arm around each one's shoulders. They looked quite comical.

'Claire won't fly either... pity you two couldn't meet. Ye'd 'ave plenty to talk about... flyin' that is.'

'Aye. I'll stay here on the ground, mate. Claire's got the right idea. Got the ground under me feet that'll do me.'

'Seems it's movin' a bit at the moment.'

''It sure is swayin' around somethin' terrible like. Maybe it's an earthquake.'

Both men started to giggle like schoolgirls.

'Will ye be havin' another spot of the whiskey?' Declan asked. 'Now what's happened here? I think we've drunk the bottle dry, brother. I'll just 'ave to drink a toast to ye with an empty glass.'

The two brothers clunked their glasses together again. Still holding each other upright, Declan announced,

'Here's to ye flyin' safe in that bloody tin box an'

arrivin' at yer destination in one piece.'

His toast brought about another bout of giggles. It was the closest the two brothers had ever been.

'I'll be leavin' ye with the problem of Mary,' said Oisin after a few seconds.

'Lucky bugger,' replied Declan. 'Ah, I have a plan. Aye, think this one might work... can ye manage to smuggle her into yer luggage?'

'Doubt if she could fit,' giggled Oisin.

'Looks like ye are leavin' me an' Joyce with the problem then, don't it now?'

And with that profound statement, both men staggered, somewhat like two shuffling penguins navigating the ice, back to the family group who by that time were as merry as they were.

There was still no sign of Mary.

****

In that grey area between sleeping and waking, Oisin stirred. His head hurt and his mouth was as dry as the Sahara, he thought as he opened an eye, and then the other one. The digital clock beside his bed read five thirty. Why had he woken up so early after the night of revelry at An Teach Ban? He had staggered home to the cabin at about one o'clock in the morning and fallen, somewhat unceremoniously onto his bed, fully clothed. His head spun when he managed, with some difficulty and a fair amount of cursing, to extract his shoes from his feet. He couldn't remember much else except he just wanted to shut his eyes and trust that the spinning head would be suitably relieved after a few hours' sleep.

It was the pounding of a fist on the cabin door and not his throbbing head that had woken him at such an early hour. Cursing under his breath, he recovered one shoe and then searched for the other one which had somehow managed to become separated from the other one and was found nestled on top of the chest of drawers in the bedroom.

'I'm comin',' he muttered under his breath. 'In the name of all that's holy, what's all the noise about? Can't a man have a decent sleep my last day in Ireland?'

He opened the door to find an animated Mary, standing there in the half-light with a tartan beret on her head and an equally fashionable red, blue and orange shawl wrapped around her shoulders.

'Christ, Mary,' he exclaimed, 'what in the name of God are ye doin' here at this hour? The feckin' cockerel isn't even awake!'

'Let me in.'

He opened the door slightly and she pushed him aside. Sat down on one of the two lounge chairs in the cabin and lit a cigarette.

'I heard you're leaving us,' she said in a rather posh voice.

'Well... of course I am. Didn't see ye at the farewell party... now did I?'

'What about *my* party?'

'None of us have seen head nor hide of ye for days. Thought ye had forgotten all about your party.' He emphasised the "your" in a rather deliberate way.

His remark seemed to have annoyed Mary. She blew some smoke in his direction and he coughed.

'Well, I had still planned on a party. Now it's ruined.' She pouted.

'Oh Mary, grow up.'

'Don't patronise me.'

'Well, it was quite a night an' I've got some helluva hangover. I'll make us some coffee an' we'll talk about it.'

Oisin, somewhat unsteady on his feet, proceeded to the small kitchenette and filled the electric kettle with a somewhat shaky hand.

'Now, where's that feckin' jar of coffee? I thought there was some somewhere.'

'It's in front of you, beside the sugar,' came a somewhat sarcastic voice.

'Oh, aye. Black coffee it'll have to be. I've no milk seein' as I'm leavin' tomorrow.'

A moment later, two coffees were made and

Oisin sat down beside his sister.

'I'm leavin' tomorrow, early,' he said. 'Catching the train from Ballybeg to Heuston Station. Staying the night with Frankie before I catch my flight.'

'Back to the great outback then?'

Oisin took a sip of his coffee. The caffeine helped. He managed to focus both his eyes onto his sister's face.

Mary stubbed her cigarette out on a saucer, took a sip of coffee, made a face for the coffee was bitter, then she said,

'I could come with you.'

'What?'

'You heard. I've never been to Australia...'

'I'm not going to Australia. Not for a while.'

It was Mary's turn to look surprised.

'Where are you going then? Thought you'd be in a hurry to get back to all that space... and your darling wife, of course.'

'Well, Claire's OK. She told me to stay for as long as it takes.'

'What do you mean? "For as long as it takes."'

'Just that.'

'Well, where are you going then? Staying in Dublin?'

'Of course not. I'd outwear my welcome very quickly with the two lovebirds.'

There was a pause while both brother and sister

took in the conversation. They finished their coffee at the same time and replaced both cups on the coffee table between the two lounge chairs.

'No, Mary,' Oisin said after a few more minutes. 'I've been doin' a lot of thinkin' these past few days. There's somewhere I must go.'

'Well?'

'I've a flight booked to Edinburgh.'

'Edinburgh?'

'Oh, aye. Edinburgh.'

Oisin did not expect the response from Mary after his reference to Edinburgh. She stood up, shook her head, 'tut tutted', and not looking at him again, walked somewhat unsteadily across the small cabin floor to the door. Then she turned and muttered,

'Edinburgh you said?'

Then she slammed the door behind her leaving her brother somewhat perplexed. Why did the mention of Edinburgh cause such a reaction?

****

The rest of Oisin's last day in Ballybeg was spent getting ready to leave. He walked further along the sea shore than he had done in years. It was his intention to capture the memory of the place, to store it into his mind and have that memory there, safely tucked away so that when he was far away, he would be able to shut his eyes and picture it all again. He breathed deeply and, in a meditative state, sat upon his favourite rock, and shut his eyes. Despite everything, Oisin Kelly did so love the sea in all its moods. He thought somewhat wryly that the sea was like his sister, Mary, unpredictable, awe inspiring and beautiful; at different times, all three. The waves crashing onto the sand were timeless and would be there when both he and Mary were gone. But he could hold the memory of the scene until his dying day.

He walked at a leisurely pace into Ballybeg to visit what had become his favourite café, *The Cat and the Fiddle*. He ordered a cappuccino and a ham and cheese Panini garnished with slices of tomato and cucumber, two lettuce leaves covered in a vinaigrette salad dressing. The waitress had got to know him and when she delivered his order, she said,

'Ye are sure lookin' thoughtful today, Oisin. So ye are.'

'I'm leavin' tomorrow,' he replied. 'My last day in Ballybeg.'

'We'll miss ye.'

'Sure, and I'll miss ye too.'

'Ye'll be back though, won't ye?'

Oisin smiled.

'Well, ye never know.'

But in his heart he knew different.

He said goodbye to Declan and Joyce, then Ryan. He knocked on Mary's cabin door but there was no answer.

****

The train to Dublin left early, at 7.30 in the morning and Oisin arrived on time. Ryan drove him into town.

'I'll say goodbye to ye out here,' Ryan said when they arrived at the station. The two men shook hands and gave each other a man hug. 'Farewells can be hard. Safe journey. Been great to get to know ye, Uncle Oisin.'

'Thanks for everything, Ryan. Look after yeself, an' say goodbye to Alice for me. Been great meetin' ye both. Glad we both made it up Slieve Gael and got back in one piece,' he grinned. 'And keep an' eye out for Mary for me, won't ye? I know she's difficult but she's me wee sister after all.' And with those final words, Oisin walked towards the station entrance and onto the platform to await the arrival of the train.

A few people waited at the station. A young mother with two young children, a boy and a girl, was doing her best to keep the children from chasing each other along the platform but the two of them, aged about eight and six, took no notice until she grabbed the boy by his collar and admonished him. The boy made a face at his sister behind his mother's back. Two nuns huddled together on one of the benches; both appeared somewhat annoyed at the children's antics. A man of about thirty dressed in a dark brown suit and holding his laptop in one hand with a small case at his feet, looked somewhat anxious. The man was focused on his phone, oblivious to what was going on around him. When Oisin turned to look in the opposite direction, and he saw who was there, he couldn't believe his eyes.

She noticed him looking at her, and she cried out in a loud voice,

'Edinburgh... you said. You are going to Edinburgh, you said. I'm coming with you whether you like it or not, Oisin.'

Everyone looked around, even the man with his phone. The children ceased their play for a brief moment and the two nuns stopped talking.

'But Mary... '

'No but's. I've booked on the same flight as you. Rang Frankie. I'll stay with him tonight and we board the plane tomorrow.'

'But...'

'I have to go to Edinburgh,' she announced. 'It's

important.'

'Why?'

Mary shrugged her shoulders, swung her handbag over her left shoulder and gave him a smile akin to the Mona Lisa's.

'Things I must do, that's why. Let's go.'

PART TWO

REVELATION

CHAPTER SIX

Anton Le Bon strolled across the Meadows with no particular plan for the day. His spirits were high for he had just spent the night with his latest woman, a University of Edinburgh lecturer in Molecular Chemistry. He had been enjoying a delightful liaison with this thirty something year old divorcee for the last six months. Neither of whom, it appeared, had any particular plans to extend their affair for longer than was necessary. Who would tire first was anyone's guess?

Anton was in no great hurry to get to his art gallery in Dundas Street. He was feeling extremely pleased. A week ago he had taken a risk and exhibited fifty oil and mixed media paintings by an up and coming young artist by the name of Francesca Fitzwilliam, whom he had the pleasure of introducing to his well-heeled clients. He knew his fellow gallery owners and a good number of the art critics were sceptical when they first saw the paintings at the opening night, and in all honesty quite a few of them would have liked to see his exhibition fail, Anton not being their most trusted competitor nor their most likeable figure, for that matter. Even Anton was surprised by the sales, at the last count only three of the paintings were left unsold. Francesca, somewhat naïve in the ways of the art world, was totally overwhelmed by the sales of her paintings. She followed Anton around like a lapdog. This youthful adoration suited the hardened businessman just fine. Francesca was attractive with her long black hair and equally long legs. In this case, gallery entrepreneur, Anton Le Bon sensed huge profits could be made from this particular artist, and also something even more delightful might come from their acquaintance, if he played his cards right.

Although now well into his sixties and his libido somewhat diminished, Anton could still admire the view. With these pleasantly sensual, and the occasional monetary thought in mind, the aging lover of many women sat down on one of the benches in the park to observe the passing parade of young students and mothers. It appeared that the two groups were competing for walking space as the mothers pushing prams, often with a toddler in tow slowed the students down. One of the toddlers, a boy of about three years of age with a mass of curly red hair, stopped right in front of Anton and stared at him with eyes that didn't appear to blink. It looked as if he was about to speak and Anton rather hoped he wouldn't. Anton was unsure of what to say to small children. He preferred the company of adults, and young woman in particular. As luck would have it, he was spared any embarrassment because at that precise moment the youngster spied a squirrel. Not hesitating, the boy released himself from his mother's hand, and with a yell of pure delight, ran after the grey squirrel, much to the exasperation of his mother. The three students almost collided with the youngster. The squirrel was up the tree in a flash. The child was not about to give up the chase. The mother, full of apology and looking slightly embarrassed, tried to rescue the child who by this time was intent on climbing the tree. The young students, happily engaged in their own world, appeared not to bother too much with the drama unfolding before them. One of the girls, however, noticed the child and his playful pursuit, and she broke away from the group. Calling out to him to catch her, she ran round and round the tree pretending to be the squirrel. The boy had just managed to get a toe hold onto the tree trunk but when he spied the girl, he lost interest in the squirrel, giggled and jumped down. The two young people chased each other round the tree a few times and then the girl re-joined her group. With a quick word to the mother, and still laughing, the three students walked on, chattering. The mother finally managed to grab the boy's hand again, pushed the pram with the baby, who by now had started to bellow, and, with a half apologetic nod to Anton followed a few paces behind the students along the path. It was an agreeable and amusing interlude for Anton, safely seated on his bench.

You would have been mistaken if you had called Anton a *voyeur* for he was not. His interest in the female form was both an appreciation of it from an artistic point of view and also a sexual one. He delighted in the pursuit of the opposite sex but it was true to say that his interest did not extend to any great long time associations with them. He had married once which proved to be a disaster to both parties and they parted ways six months after they tied the knot. And then there was a rumour that he lived with one of his young female artists for a longer time than that, maybe four years or so, but no one was too sure of the veracity of this. Anton Le Bon could be rather discreet in matters of the heart.

****

To say that Oisin was pleased with his sister's unexpected announcement that she was to accompany him to Edinburgh was something of an understatement. In fact, the usual phlegmatic Irishman was furious. He felt as if his own plans were now put in jeopardy because he would be duty bound to look out for Mary whose moods swings and unpredictable behaviour were becoming more and more of a worry. He had no idea why she had all of a sudden decided to leave Ballybeg and come with him. He was even more annoyed with her because she had taken it upon herself to stay the night with Frankie and had somehow managed to book a seat on the same flight from Dublin to Edinburgh. He sulked all the way on the train journey to Dublin, and by the time the two siblings found their way to Frankie's modest dwelling in the seaside suburb of Bray, he was even surlier. Frankie and Ellen did their best to be welcoming but it was an awkward evening all round. Mary, for her part, seemed oblivious to the situation. She talked non-stop. No mention was made as to why she had decided to travel to Edinburgh until Frankie, who by virtue of his big brother status always considered himself to be the leader in the family, asked a direct question to which Mary replied airily that she had always wanted to visit the Scottish capital and had been annoyed with Oisin all her life because when they were young, he had refused to let her join him on his mission to the city as directed by their Uncle Mick. No one had heard from Oisin for over forty years after that trip, concluded Mary. Indeed apart from their recent reunion, the last time she had seen Oisin was when they were teenagers in Ballybeg which was almost a lifetime in her opinion. Now it was his turn to make amends and show her the sights of Edinburgh. Everyone looked to Oisin for an answer.

'I hadn't intended to sight see', he replied and shrugged his shoulders.

'What are ye going to do over there then?' asked a somewhat surprised Frankie.

'This and that.'

'Always full of secrets, aren't you, Oisin?' Mary glared at him.

Oisin shrugged his shoulders once more. He had no intention of telling any of them what his plans were in Edinburgh. That was the end of the conversation as far as he was concerned. He excused himself early and went to bed.

****

Oisin was still out of sorts with Mary when the plane made its descent over the Forth to the Edinburgh Airport. Fortunately, Mary hadn't been able to secure a seat next to him so he had been able to try to work out a plan as what to do with her when they arrived in the capital. He wasn't sure where they would spend their first night. It had been forty years since he had lived there. There were bound to be changes.

Much to his surprise, Mary seemed to have decided that they would stay at a Bed and Breakfast not far from Arthur's Seat. She had already booked two rooms online. Her plan was to stay there a week and then look around for somewhere to rent on a short term let.

'How did you know I would ask ye to come with me?' Oisin asked her. He was still furious.

'You owe me.'

'But why, Mary? Ye know how it all worked out. I met the Luchettas and Concetta, Mick's daughter in Edinburgh. That's what Mick wanted me to do. There was no way ye could have come with me, ye were still at school.'

Mary shrugged.

'Remember, Silvio Luchetta used to come over to Ballybeg and meet with Mick. None of us knew then that Mick had a daughter and that he had been involved with Silvio's sister.'

'Well, we're here now. It's time to make amends. And I have things to do here,' she added and she frowned.

Oisin was puzzled. The Mary he had got to know over the last two months wasn't the Mary of his childhood. They used to be such mates then. Of course, everyone in the family spoiled her but being the youngest two, they had had such fun together sometimes. Fond memories of riding their ponies along the strand and all manner of discussions between them, they were two young adventurers all set to conquer the world. At least, that's what it had felt like then until life got in the way and reality set in. He knew nothing about her life these past forty years. Had she had any relationships? Had she married or even lived with anyone? She was tight lipped whenever he tried to broach the subject. And why was there such animosity between Mary and her mother? Mother and daughter should have got on. Then there was her art. She had a talent there. Everyone knew this and the Protestant minister in Ballybeg, Reverend Williamson had tried to encourage her, he being a water colourist of sorts. Again, Mary never spoke about her art. It seemed that all he had heard about Mary since he had been in Ballybeg was her mental state. And he had been on the receiving end of this a few times. The nurse, Seamus O'Maera had cautioned him and warned him that she was stable if she kept to her medication. Oisin was somewhat reticent to ask Mary whether she followed the medical advice on this matter. He feared if he said anything about it, he might receive a torrent of abuse from her, and even physical harm, the umbrella incident was often on his mind. It was an altogether worrying situation for him. Now they were in Edinburgh together, and neither knew what the other one was planning to do, or even thinking about.

'Well, we'd better find this B and B,' he said after a few moments. 'Least we've got a bed for a week.'

'Oh, Oisin. You're such a worrier.' And she gave him a quick peck on the cheek as if nothing had happened between them. This unexpected physical contact further confused an already puzzled Oisin.

'Oh, well, let's go then,' he said. He spied their luggage coming along at a fast rate on the carousel. 'Looks like we both have things to do here, doesn't it?'

****

Having spent more than an hour sitting on his bench in the Meadows and enjoying the passing parade of young and not so young women, Anton Le Bon strolled into his favourite coffee house, sat down at his usual seat and ordered a flat white coffee. Anton was well known in the establishment and his habits were regular. He always ordered the same coffee at the same time every morning. He insisted the coffee be brought to him in a large cup and saucer and, on different occasions, he would request a slice of apple tart or sample one of the delicious looking cakes that were displayed at the counter. Other diners lined up at the counter to be served. This was not Anton. When he first discovered the coffee house and noticed the queue, he called for the manager. The resulting discussion resulted in Anton being offered the best table in the room with an assurance that he would be waited on in the future. Queuing for Anton was something the peasants did. The manager, no doubt noticing the expensive suit and the silk cravat, decided then and there that here was a customer worth cultivating. So began Anton Le Bon's attachment to the place.

Today things were different, however. Anton's usual table was occupied by a rather stout gentleman of about fifty years of age, and sitting opposite him, looking rather surly, was an equally plump woman companion of about the same age. The two were engaged in what seemed to be, a heated conversation, and when Anton approached their table neither of them took any notice.

'I think you are seated at my table,' announced Anton in his usual manner.

The stout gentleman looked up and when he saw Anton, he laughed.

'I think I know you,' he said. 'Why, bless me it's... Anton Le Bon, of all people.'

Turning to his companion he said, 'You remember Anton, my dear.'

'I don't think so,' replied the woman. She glanced at Anton and then quickly looked away. He noticed that a red flush had travelled from her neck towards her cheeks.

'Of course you do,' insisted the man. 'I

remember you had quite an attachment to Mr Le Bon, didn't you, dear... all those years ago?'

'I'm sorry to say that I don't know you,' said Anton. He looked slightly uncomfortable. He glanced at the woman and turned away from her to focus entirely on the man's face. 'And you are still at my table.'

By now, the woman was completely ill at ease. She stuffed the remaining piece of iced fruit cake into her mouth and emptied her cup with a gulp.

'I think we'd better go, Howard,' she muttered to the man. She got up without looking at Anton, and wiped her lips on the paper serviette.

Her companion, who was obviously her husband, wasn't about to give up. He remained seated.

'I will join you shortly, my dear. Outside,' he said. 'After I finish my coffee...'

Turning now to Anton, he continued,

'Ah, Anton Le Bon, the famous gallery owner.'

This was said with a slight touch of sarcasm.

'You must remember my wife, Harriet. In her day, she was a talented artist. I thought you would recognise her even though she's put on a bit of weight since then.'

There followed a tense pause before the man continued,

'My wife managed to sell a lot of her paintings,

and I'm sure you will recall that one of her exhibitions was held at your gallery... in London.'

'I've exhibited many talented artists. I can't recall the name,' Anton mumbled. Now to anyone watching the scene unfold, he appeared to be somewhat embarrassed which was unusual for Anton. He rarely allowed himself to be put into difficult situations. This was one of them.

'But you *do* remember Harriet, Mr Le Bon. She was somewhat in awe of you, I recall. Then we moved up north to Scotland soon after the exhibition at your gallery. You must remember the circumstances of our move. Harriet gave it all up for me and the children when they arrived, you know. But you would know that, wouldn't you?'

Anton Le Bon was rarely at a loss for words but on this occasion, he gave the impression that he wished to be anywhere but where he was, and the table that was always reserved for him, was of little consequence. He needed to escape from the man's stare but he still wanted his usual coffee. His mouth had become surprisingly dry. A strong cup of black coffee was required as a matter of some urgency, he thought. His usual flat white could wait until tomorrow.

'I will leave you to your coffee then,' replied a red-faced Anton and, without another glance, he joined the queue lining up at the counter.

It was then that the manager saw him.

'Why, Mr Le Bon,' he said. 'I do apologise. My new staff member wasn't aware that your table was always reserved for you. It won't happen again, I can assure you. Would you care to join me in my office for a coffee to your liking? No charge, of course.'

It has to be noted that at that point, the Anton of so many words, was more than relieved that he had been rescued from what had become for him, a very awkward situation at that particular moment in time.

'That would be most acceptable,' he mumbled with a slight smile which was also unusual for Anton. He rarely smiled. 'Just a misunderstanding all round, I believe.'

****

A slight gap in the curtain sent a sliver of oblong light onto the bed and Oisin stirred. He opened his eyes and looked around the small room. His bed was positioned close to the window and he could hear the hum from outside traffic. At midnight he had been awakened to the sound of an ambulance. The blue lights from the vehicle reflected through the thin curtain onto the wall. The blinking and then the noise from its siren seeming to split open the dark night. Still half asleep, he heard a police vehicle sped by followed by more traffic. He woke fully with the hiss of the brakes of a bus outside his window. As people got out of the bus there was even more noise. He sighed. A few minutes later what seemed to be a heavy vehicle stopped behind the bus and he heard the driver changing gears. He got out of the bed and opened the curtain to see what was happening but all was quieter in the street apart from another slow moving lorry, a black Edinburgh taxi, and the bark of a dog.

He sunk back down on the bed under the duvet cover with its pink and red rose pattern, and rested his head on the pillow case with its matching floral design. Everything in the room was laid out to perfection but it wasn't a homely sort of place, rather it was a functional room, tidy, clean and devoid of any lived in look. It was just what it was. He was glad he was only staying in the room for a little while. After that, he hoped that his mission to Edinburgh would be over and he could head back to Kilgoolga and Claire. However, now he was uncertain of his next move for he had his sister to contend with. Still annoyed with her, he was at a loss to think what her plans were and why she had even wanted to come with him. It couldn't just be because of his escape from Ballybeg all those years ago to Edinburgh. Surely, she couldn't hold a grudge about that and about him for all that time, but given her irrationality, he could only wonder.

Sleep eluded him for the next hour or so for his mind was all a muddle with too many thoughts and images that jostled for space in his mind. His decision to return to Edinburgh had been something of a whim. As he tossed and turned in the uncomfortable bed, and trying as best he could to block out the noise from the now constant swish of traffic outside his window, his thoughts turned to doubts and then to questions. Nostalgia, he decided was an altogether tantalising emotion for we can never recapture the past no matter how hard we strive for it. We take photographs of our holidays, our children growing up, and all those significant events that we so desperately want to hang on to, all these things, but we can never be back there again, no matter how hard we try. Maybe his desire to return to Edinburgh was like that. For his rational self knew that the time there as it had been was over, had been over for forty years or so. The past was the past, and the life he lived in Edinburgh was gone just like his youth. With that sobering thought in mind, he shut his eyes and the much longed for sleep came to him at last.

He opened his eyes about seven o'clock to the sound of a city waking up. The day time traffic sound had become louder. His room was positioned just a few metres away from the bus stop. The voices from people and the constant stopping and starting of the buses finally woke him. It took him a few moments to work out where he was for city noises were foreign to him now. All was peace and quiet at Ryan's place. The honking and flapping of wings from the gaggle of geese and the two resident cockerels competing for space had been his early morning call there. Ballybeg, for all the eco rebirth was still a country town in the west of Ireland. Then he had lived for forty years in outback Australia with the kookaburras and the magpies to awaken him. No wonder the city felt noisy and even turning his deaf ear to the sounds made little difference. He could still hear the noise. He sighed, stretched and got out of bed.

All his life his morning routine had been much the same. We are all creatures of habit and Oisin was no different. The water from the bathroom tap was icy cold. He shaved, looking at the face that peered out at him from the small but adequate bathroom mirror. Furrow lines and grey hair, thinning now, he was getting older.

He smiled at himself in the mirror as he ran a comb through his once curly hair. Not so many curls now, and that hair was disappearing at a rapid rate from his forehead.

Least he was still active, he thought, for he had

much to do.

He dressed quickly for the room was cool even though it was spring. The landlady obviously didn't want to spend money on heating rooms for her guests. Edinburgh seemed colder than Ballybeg. He decided to wear the navy blue and brown striped polo neck that Claire had knitted for him to keep him warm. There was always a comforting connection to her when he put it on. A sudden pang of loneliness came over him. He missed her and the heat of Kilgoolga at that particular moment.

Mary's room was next to his and he tapped gently on the door. There was no answer and he tapped harder. Still no answer. She might be having breakfast, he thought as he made his way downstairs to the dining room. The varnished English oak sideboard positioned alongside the wall nearest the door, and set out on top of it and under a lace cloth were table napkins and cutlery, all arranged with careful attention, everything there necessary for serving breakfast, this could have been a dining room in a dozen similar establishments. The sideboard looked rather out of place as if this was a family heirloom set amongst the cheaper looking tables and chairs and should not have to be in the same room as the lesser furniture. He sat down at a table set out for two next to the sideboard and studied the carvings of flowers, thistles and leaves which adorned its two doors and three drawers. The carvings were precise and beautifully executed. This had been a master woodcarver at work. Oisin had made his living working with wood and he admired quality work. He wondered whether he should complement the B and B owner when she appeared.

Mary was nowhere to be seen. He was alone in the room except for a middle aged couple who had finished their breakfast and were about to leave. As they passed by his table, the man said to him, 'Gidday, mate. Bit chilly out there.' and the woman giggled. 'Too right', she said. 'We're not used to the cold. But it's lovely here. Everything's so old. Not like Australia.' Oisin nodded as a way of acknowledgment. He had no desire to tell these strangers that he was almost an Australian. He thought of Claire. His wife was still in his head alongside the dust and the never ending distances. Australia was old, too, but in an altogether different way.

The couple left the room and Oisin sat there wondering where on earth Mary was. The B and B owner appeared, trying to be as friendly as she possibly could, although Oisin judged her friendliness would vanish as soon as the guests left and her home was hers again. She was a tiny woman. She resembled a small bird in flight for she darted here and there around the room. Her mousey, rather untidy hair was loosely secured behind her ears in a sort of bun, and what with her rimless glasses balancing on the end of her nose; she looked for all the world like a 1950's stereotypical schoolmarm. When he managed to catch her eye, he asked had his sister been for breakfast.

'Oh, aye,' she said. 'The lady was the first to be served. She had things to do, she said and had to be off early.'

'Did she say where she was headed?'

'Not a mention. I dinnae like to enquire to my guests as to what they're doing. Some like to talk, never a peep out of others. Meet all sorts, ye do. Nay, your sister was one of them what don't want to talk so I just let her be. Dinnae eat much either, just a slice of toast and tea.'

'I don't think she's ever been in Edinburgh before,' Oisin said but then he didn't know. For all he knew about Mary, she could have lived in the place for years. 'But guess she's old enough to know what she's doing.' He managed a weak smile.

'Oh aye. Right dressed up she was too. I admired her cashmere cardigan... we've great woollen mills in the Borders, you know. I used to live down there in Innerleithen so I ken a wee bit about knitting and wool... but she didn't seem to

139

want to talk about it, so I just held me tongue. I got the impression that your sister knows her own mind an' wouldn't take kindly to takin' advice... least not from the likes of me.'

'Oh aye. That's Mary alright.'

They were silent for a few moments as each thought what to say next. The B and B owner broke the silence first with the safe option to enquire as to his preferences for breakfast. A slightly relieved Oisin replied that he would like the full Scottish with a pot of tea, and definitely some porridge to begin with.

'You'll be having the Scottish porridge then,' was the reply. 'With salt, nay sugar. It's the Sassenachs what have the sugar, ye ken.'

Then, seeing a slightly puzzled look on the Irishman's face, she added, 'But I'll be puttin' some sugar on the table for ye, just in case.'

And she beat a somewhat hasty retreat in the direction of her kitchen leaving Oisin to ponder once again what his sister was up to, and what he should do on this, his first day in Scotland's capital, and if Scottish porridge tasted different from the Irish.

Later that morning with his hunger satisfied after eating a very generous serving of porridge followed by the full Scottish, tea and toast, Oisin Kelly, dressed for the Edinburgh spring day by putting on a dark brown well-worn rain coat over Claire's decorative woollen jumper. His light blue denim jeans, slightly threadbare at the knees were still appropriate for a man his age, he decided, and the sturdy walking boots he'd bought years before in Sydney, completed his outfit. Suitably attired, he stepped out into the street to the blast of noise and traffic. He had no clear plan as to what to do for the day but he hoped that he could recover something of his earlier equilibrium. Somehow, and he knew not how, his past was about to be relived.

Almost at the same time, and in another part of town, Anton Le Bon after continuing his leisurely stroll from the Meadows, then to the coffee lounge, was in the process of unlocking the door to his gallery. Unlike Oisin, Anton Le Bon had a clear plan of how his day should work out.

CHAPTER SEVEN

Anton Le Bon was still thinking of the encounter in the coffee lounge with the fat and abrupt woman and her equally distasteful husband as he approached his gallery. For the life of him, he couldn't remember the woman. Neither her face nor her figure bore any resemblance to anyone he remembered, and as for the man, he was a nameless individual of little importance. If it was true that there had been some sort of liaison between himself and the woman, it must surely have been nothing more than a one night stand. Had she exhibited paintings at his gallery, it would have been in the days when he was making a name for himself and her work would have been one of the many aspiring young female artists who came to his door begging for recognition. As for the alleged relationship, this worried him because he normally kept track of his affairs if they lasted more than a few days. It did look as if there had been some sort of relationship between the fat one and himself by the actions of the couple. The woman had been embarrassed and beat a hasty retreat from the coffee lounge and her husband was certainly hostile. Most of the time, Anton steered clear of cuckolded husbands and if he had been tempted to stray into that particular area, the woman must have been a looker, and worth it, not in any way like the woman he had just encountered. Then again, time does things to people and beautiful women grow old. Anton thought the best course was just to forget the whole uncomfortable incident. After all, he had known a lot of women. Not all of them had been worth remembering.

He fumbled in his pocket for the key to open the door of his art gallery. The elevated sign with letters written in gold plate spelled out the rather pretentious name of *Le Bon*. To label the gallery with his surname was a move he had made deliberately. His view had been that he was famous enough within the art community, and beyond, that his name alone over the door was enough. There was no need to add the word 'Gallery'. The absence of this definitive noun would annoy his rivals but further enhance his reputation amongst the art buying populace. Everyone who was anyone would be able to say: *'Have you seen the latest exhibits at Le Bon? Why, the man's a genius. What talent he discovers.'* All this had been done when he first set his sights on conquering the Scottish art scene some twenty years before. At that time he viewed his move from London to Edinburgh as something of a provincial step backwards. However Anton, first and foremost, was one of those ambitious, and it has to be said, ruthless businessmen who would stop at nothing nor let anyone block their way in achieving their success. Had he not immersed himself in conquering the elitists and the namedroppers who regularly attended openings of his galleries, he would have fitted quite happily into the role of a car salesman. Selling was everything to Anton, Success with a capital 'S' being the ultimate goal, because success for the entrepreneurial businessman meant money, with a capital 'M'. Anton Le Bon adored money.

It was that money that had given him a ten bedroom mansion in Surrey complete with swimming pool and tennis court set in three acres, a yacht moored in the Mediterranean on the island of Mallorca, although it has to be noted that the said yacht was much smaller than the ones owned by the billionaires anchored in the vicinity. Anton was a millionaire but not quite in the category of the super-rich although if you could get into his mind, perhaps being able to afford a super yacht and so mingle with associated persons was another of his ambitions. Along with yacht and mansion, there was a small and secluded apartment in Bologna and a townhouse in Edinburgh. With all these properties, one would have thought that Anton would be satisfied but the acquisition for more and more was to him something of a passion as it is to so many like himself. He pursued material things with resolute determination and when he set his sights on something, whether it be property, art or beautiful women, nothing would stand in his way.

Sometimes, however the passion turned into an obsession and needed to be curtailed. This happened when a down turn in profits happened for not all the Le Bon galleries were successful. Then Anton's accountant would advise that the best course was to sell some of his assets and thus wait until the market picked up again. The ten bedroom mansion in Surrey had been the one to go along with a gallery in London as well. Funds were then directed to the other remaining gallery in London where the clientele were more inclined to part with their cash. As he now spent a good part of the year in Edinburgh the decision to sell both properties was an astute business plan as well as a personal one. He had grown quite fond of living in the city so buying a house with a sizable garden in a leafy suburb of Edinburgh with the proceeds from the sale of the Surrey mansion suited his somewhat changed lifestyle just fine. He planned that the Edinburgh house and garden would be something of a retreat for him as now approaching sixty five he was beginning to tire of travelling to his various galleries around the globe. Although one place he had become a frequent visitor of late was New York. The entrepreneurial fire and the lust for more and more were not totally extinguished within him for the millionaire gallery owner had no desire to sit back and retire with all his wealth if there were more to be made. Amassing money was something he still desired and with the steely resolve that had made his fortune, Anton drew up plans to open a gallery in San Francisco with the same name, *Le Bon*. He had dipped his toe into America when he opened his New York gallery. This gallery situated near to Central Park was a success. The rich and the famous bought art and he quickly became known but he still wasn't satisfied. He wanted to conquer America and if a gallery in New York and the other one in San Francisco attracted the super-rich who would certainly be persuaded by any means to frequent his galleries, the dream of a super yacht might just be his!

With that enticing thought in mind, Anton entered his Edinburgh gallery to be met by his gallery manager, a rather surprising individual by the name of Martin MacDonald. The physical characteristics between the two men could not have been more dissimilar. Anton was a short and stocky with a perfectly trimmed goatee beard. Both the hair on his face and the hair on his head were turning grey whilst the hair on his head was disappearing at an alarming rate as if its sole purpose was to catch up with the bald patch on the top of his head.

Martin MacDonald was twenty years younger than Anton and a good eighteen inches taller. The clean shaven Martin and his mass of unruly curly red hair gave the impression of a Highland chieftain of old. When the two men first met Anton had not been impressed for Martin showed no signs of being the sycophant that the gallery entrepreneur was used to. But not being obsequious proved to be a blessing. Martin knew his own mind, had a keen sense of business acumen, could charm the pants off any potential buyer, sort out problem clients and keep Anton's diary up to date. It was an association that had lasted ten years and showed no signs of coming to an end. Another factor between the two men was that Martin knew of his employer's dalliances and turned a blind eye to them, discretion being sacrosanct in this case although the gallery manager was amused by the number of women who graced Anton's bed and who disappeared from there at sometimes lightning speed, although it has to be said, some lasted longer than others. Women seemed drawn to Anton like moths to the proverbial flame and Martin, like so many others speculated as to why this was so. What was his secret? Was it the money? Or the charm? Anton could put on the charm when he wanted to, and even if that charm wore off after a time, women still appeared to regard the aging lothario with fondness even after the inevitable parting of the ways. Some of his women remained his friend and would visit him and invite him to dinner or go to the theatre. However, on the occasion that the relationship soured to such an extent that it was the woman who gave Anton the boot, he wasn't quite so charitable. Then his true nature surfaced and the black moods and bad temper was much in evidence until a new lady was found. At first Martin took some delight in ticking off the number of women but now, after ten years, he had lost interest. There were just too many to be bothered with. Martin was happily married with two children, a boy with a mass of red hair and a daughter with the same colour hair and freckles to match. No two men could have been more different, but it worked.

Martin was busy on his laptop when Anton entered the room and he didn't greet his employer straight away, just gave a cursory nod. He frowned as he tapped away at the keys. Martin definitely had something on his mind. It was not in Anton's nature to interrupt his manager-cum-secretary when that particular man was so absorbed. A keen observer of human nature, at least as far as his employees and potential buyers were concerned, Anton knew by the look on Martin's face that something important was being uncovered in the wonderful world of cyber space, the discovery of a new artist or perhaps more satisfying, a sale in six figures? So Anton roamed around the vast room that was *Le Bon* and took a careful note of the paintings on display and the presence of a few more red dots. Francesca Fitzwilliam was doing him proud. He made money; the artist made art, and in the case of Francesca, art and just enough money to pay her bills with a little left over.

Le Bon comprised two vast studio spaces with paintings on the walls and sculptures arranged on display in one room whilst the other room usually held exhibitions of other creative endeavours, pottery, wood and glass with sometimes fabric exhibitions if the right artist was found; the lesser room Anton thought. But he had learned to diversify and sales could be made just as easily in the lesser, smaller room. In fact, he had recently sold a huge decorative burr elm bowl for a four figure sum from this very room. Life brought many surprises, Anton thought and the lesser room often brought in more sales than the larger, more pretentious front room.

Anton's pleasant pondering was disturbed when he heard Martin call out from behind the desk. The Scotsman rarely showed much emotion but in this case, he sounded positively beside himself.

'Anton. We've done it. Out of the blue, we've done it.' Martin shook his fist in the air, stood up to his full height and let out a cry that can only be described as one of pure joy. 'You'd better see this, boss. Can't quite believe it.'

The laptop revealed a surprise for there on the screen for all to see was a bank transfer for the six foot high bronze that graced the front room.

The giant bronze depicted the naked body of Prometheus, lying back down on jaggy rocks, arms outstretched as if he was pinned to a crucifix and his taut and muscular body held down by chains whilst an eagle straddled his chest with its massive wings unfolded, threatening to kill the supine figure. The large talons of the bird pieced his victim's body. The fierce beak was poised and ready to tear out the liver of the god of fire. It was a monumental piece of work that had taken the sculptor four years to complete. Prometheus became a feature to the gallery and had stood there for a number of years with no buyer willing to pay the high prize for it. Once a public-funded gallery had approached Anton with a much reduced offer but no deal was struck between them and so Prometheus remained. He was even given a nickname, *Promy* and the fierce raptor became *Ernie the Eagle*.

The creator of this masterpiece was an introverted Frenchman who lived somewhere in the

Auvergne region of France. Somewhat of a recluse and considered a genius by the art critics, he lived for his art and, although his works stood in many public buildings and private homes, he had little interest in money, unlike Anton. In fact, after the initial and difficult job of coaxing Prometheus through the doors of *Le Bon*, which had taken six hefty men to accomplish, the sculptor had shown no inclination to track the sale of the bronze. Anton had not heard from him for years.

Although part of the statue was not quite as worn as the nose on Greyfriars Bobby, the beloved dog of Edinburgh, people seemed attracted to the bronze in the gallery and they liked to stroke the chain that secured Prometheus as if by doing this they could release him from the eagle and captivity. In time, with all this rubbing part of the chain uncovered the beautiful bronze underneath, just like Bobby's nose. To have found a buyer for this impressive work of art was something of a coup for both Anton and his secretary.

'*Ernie* and *Promy* are bidding us farewell as soon as a shipment can be arranged. Never expected to see them go... off to Italy, Promy, old son... it's not Greece mind... but a bit closer to home for you. Now, what do you think of that?' Martin addressed both Anton and the sculpture. He was jubilant. He had rather disliked the bronze but had felt it prudent not to express that opinion out aloud, and especially not to his boss today. Anton was set to make a tidy sum from the sale.

'Who has bought it?' asked Anton.

'A Countess di Laguna from Bologna.'

There are times in our lives when an unexpected remark catches us by surprise and the significance of it is only known to ourselves. This was one of those moments for Anton Le Bon. Had his secretary noticed the sharp intake of breath and the slight frown that passed across the brow of his employer and disappeared just as quickly, he would have been mystified but at that precise moment Martin MacDonald was too busy searching for an address on his laptop.

'Ah, found it,' he announced. 'It's to go to a Countess Sophia di Laguna at the Villa Rosa, in the Colli district of Bologna.'

Hearing the all familiar ping of an incoming email at that precise moment, Martin opened his inbox and shook his head. He appeared somewhat puzzled by its contents.

'It's from the Countess Laguna's secretary, Anton,' he said. 'The countess apparently wants to oversee the shipment of the sculpture and is flying to Edinburgh next week. She hopes that you will be available to discuss further matters with her. A reply is required as soon as possible.'

The frown that had appeared on Anton Le Bon's brow arrived back, and this time it wasn't in such a hurry to leave. He looked visibly shaken but his secretary was so intent on reading the email that he hardly noticed. It was also opening time for the gallery and a few faces were already appearing at the door waiting to be allowed in.

'How will I reply, boss?'

By this time Anton had regained some of his composure. His reply was brief.

'Tell the countess that I will be available and look forward to her visit.'

There were now five people outside. A tall man in a tweed jacket kept looking at his watch and pointing to the sign which listed the opening hours.

'Then you had better let that lot outside in before they break the door down.'

A second later, he said, 'No need. Looks like Clara's out there with a key. Just get that email out, Martin. I'll be in my office and I don't want to be disturbed.'

Clara worked at the gallery and was generally considered an asset to the place. She was a lively thirty years old and knew just how to persuade a reluctant buyer to part with their cash. Between Martin MacDonald and Clara, sales just kept coming. Perhaps one day Anton Le Bon might just decide to retire?

'Time wasters the lot of them,' grumbled Anton as he escaped to his office to think about what had just occurred.

****

Anton sat behind his desk and stared at the clock on the wall in front of him. Although his eyes were fixed upon the clock, his mind was strolling along the Via dell'Indipendenza hand in hand with Sophia Caputo. He was twenty years of age and in love. Under his arm he held a portfolio of his drawings for the two young lovers were off to see Sophia's Uncle Giovanni, an art dealer. Anton, the art student, was full of excitement. He had shown Sophia his sketches a few days before and she was enthusiastic.

'I arrange for you to meet my uncle, Anton. Uncle Giovanni is a famous man in Bologna and all of Italy. You show him your drawings and you become his protégé. Then we will be together always.'

Sophia and Anton met quite by accident a few weeks before. He had wandered along a side street in order to avoid being jostled by the crowds on the main thoroughfare and in so doing lost his bearings. Feeling slightly confused and now quite weary, he noticed a small and intimate coffee establishment and in broken Italian he ordered a black coffee. As he sipped the dark liquid and studied his map he became aware of the stranger at the next table. She was about his own age with black hair to her shoulders and a face that the artist in him would have loved to paint. With a high brow and cheekbones to match, this young woman was a beauty. Anton took a deep breath, coughed slightly and said,

'Mi scusi, signora, può... indicarmi.... direct me to.... la Galleria d'Arte Nazionale?'

He felt his face redden.

'Sí,' she replied and then in perfect English she said, 'you are very lost. I will show you on the map.'

And with that she sat down at his table and proceeded to explain the best way for him to get to the National Art Gallery of Bologna. She was so near to him and his heart beat faster. The whiff of her perfume invaded his whole being. He took another deep breath and asked whether he could impose on her for a few moments of her time? Could she walk with him to la Galleria d'Arte Nazionale?

'Sí, of course. Come. We will walk together.'

They strolled to the Piazza Maggiore, not quite hand in hand but close enough for Anton to want to hold her. Desire rose within him and the sights all around were nothing to the excitement that he felt just walking beside this young woman. She was lively and she chatted away, pointing out the best places to dine, the best shops, the quirky medieval sights of this old city. Inside la Galleria d'Arte Nazionale Anton absorbed the genius of the old masters work, Giotto's polyptych, Titian's Bacchus and Ariadne, Raphael, Giorgio Vasari, Tintoretto.

'How I wish I could paint like the Old Masters?' he murmured.

'It was a different time,' Sophia said and gave his hand a little squeeze. Then she was silent beside these great masterpieces of human endeavour, the like of which will never be seen again. After they left the gallery, he took her hand.

'May I see you again?' he asked. 'Maybe we could dine at one of the restaurants that you mentioned?'

She laughed then.

'Perhaps we should introduce ourselves?'

He was slightly embarrassed then. He was usually rather polite in matters such as this. It must have been because she had the most beautiful hazel eyes that he had ever seen and those eyes seemed to see right into his very soul. Those eyes made him forget everything.

'Sorry,' he murmured. 'Anton Le Bon, Signora. Would you do me the honour of dining with me tonight? 'And with the words, he bowed slightly and kissed her hand like the Italians do.

'I am called Sophia Caputo. Of course I accept your invitation, Anton Le Bon.'

And she kissed him on the cheek. That was the moment his whole life changed.

They dined that evening and drank too much red wine, staggered like two drunken sailors into the crowded street and held each other so as not to fall.

'My parents have an apartment here in Bologna,' she said. 'They are in Marseille and it is Giorgio's night off. Would you like some coffee?'

The apartment was spacious with a view over the old city. They drank the strongest black coffee Anton had ever tasted and made love on an enormous bed under Egyptian white cotton sheets the like of which he had never seen. Everything in the apartment signified wealth, good taste and above all the most luxurious living imaginable. The young Anton was as captivated by the surroundings as he was with the beautiful woman lying beside him. If a moment could last forever, this was one of those times. Sophia stirred and kissed him on his chest. They made love again.

After what seemed an eternity of pleasure, she leapt from the bed and announced that she would like to see his sketches sometime.

'We are an artistic family, Anton. My parents collect art and I take you to meet my Uncle Giovanni

Luigini ... he is the brother of my mother... ... and he is the most famous art dealer in all of Italy. If he likes your work, he may help you. Then you stay in Italy and we make love all day.'

'When would I have time to paint?'

'On Sunday. It will be your day off.'

'Oh, Sophia. How would I have the energy to paint?'

'On Sunday you paint me. Then you find you have the energy. It is a miracle. Poof.. and the energy comes. Sí?'

It sounded like the perfect idea.

'Tomorrow I take you to Uncle Giovanni. And you bring your drawings. Now, we sleep.'

The next morning they strolled, hand in hand to where Uncle Giovanni lived in an apartment in the old part of town. After the introductions were made, the art dealer, a shrewd man with hazel eyes like Sophia's, a nose that seemed to cover half his face and a head devoid of much hair, spoke in English,

'Now, Sophia. You tell to me that this young man is an artist. May I see your work, young man?'

'I am an art student, sir. Not really an artist.'

'We will see. Your drawings, per favore.'

Uncle Giovanni wore his spectacles around his neck held by a gold chain and when he positioned those spectacles onto his nose, he looked rather comical, like a wise old owl, thought Anton. Each sketch was studied with care. Anton's mind started to wander. It seemed like an age before Uncle Giovanni closed the sketch pad and placed it carefully back inside the leather bound case. All his movements were meticulous. He was not a man to be hurried. He sat back in his chair, replaced the spectacles onto his chest and stared at the young Anton.

'I see you have some talent, young man,' he said after a few minutes. One question... what do you desire most in life?'

At that particular moment, the only desire in Anton's mind was for the body of Sophia and to be back in the luxury of expensive sheets and that enormous bed. When he didn't answer Uncle Giovanni repeated the question and this time, he sounded a trifle irritated.

'Money.' Anton answered without hesitation.

'Money?'

'Well, to be rich. I want to be a rich man.'

'Not an artist then?'

'I didn't say that.'

'Young man, you want to be a rich man, that's what you said.'

'Yes.'

'You have talent but not enough to make you a rich man. I suggest you make your money from the talent of others.'

'How do I do that?'

'I was an artist in my youth,' Uncle Giovanni laughed. 'Then I observed that the wealth belonged to the gallery owner and the art dealer. So, I put away my easel and studied the art market and the artists. You see, with a little effort I sold art that has made my fortune. You, sir, are an entrepreneur, not an artist.'

****

And that is how it began. Anton leaned back in his chair the way Uncle Giovanni had done so all those years ago. Still with his eyes fixed on the clock on the wall of his office, he thought of Sophia di Laguna once again. For over forty years every September without fail he had travelled to Bologna to be with her when the count was away sailing with one of his boyfriends. Discretion being the better part of valour, they had grown old together and now for the first time, Sophia was coming to him. Never before had she expressed any desire to see him in either England or Scotland.

There are fifty-two weeks in every year. Two weeks of a year belonged to them alone. Those two glorious weeks they always spent in the apartment he purchased in Bologna when he made his first significant profit from the work of other artists.

'Ah, Sophia,' he murmured out aloud.

CHAPTER EIGHT

As Oisin retraced his steps on his nostalgic trip around the city of Edinburgh, he was a very thoughtful man. Tourists were already in evidence as he neared Princes Street, and what with all their back packs and suitcases, they were competing for space on the pavements with the locals. Oisin did not feel like a tourist but nor did he feel he belonged there anymore. His memory of Edinburgh was bittersweet. He had enjoyed being in the city as a young man when all was new to him. Here in the city of his youth he had been freed from all the old constraints of Ballybeg and the narrow view of life that had been his childhood. It had been a heady experience. Now it all seemed so different. But then, he was a different man than the lovesick young Irishman with his American sweetheart, Cecy. Forty years ago he had trod these streets. There was bound to be change.

It was a perfect late spring day and the world that had lain dormant all the long winter had well and truly emerged from the dark slumber. This pleased him as he tried as best he could to avoid the crowds. As he made his way towards the relative peace of the Princes Street Gardens where he planned to sit for a while and try to formulate a plan as to what he should do next, and how on earth he could locate his sister, Mary, in a city where everyone was in such a hurry, a large burly German with a loud voice waylaid him just before Scott's Monument.

'Excuse me,' the German bellowed, 'we are lost.'

A tiny woman whose head barely reached to her partner's chest, nodded in agreement.

'We arrive late last night,' she said as if that justified the fact that they had lost their way.

'See. See.' The German thrust his phone under Oisin's nose. The GPS tracker showed their position exactly.

'Where are ye headin'?' asked Oisin and he took a step backwards as both the large German and the diminutive woman were encroaching on his space. The couple stepped forward again so Oisin was almost pinned onto the metal railings near to the monument with people now jostling for space on all sides of him.

'I'm a stranger here myself,' he said to the Germans in a hope that they might get the hint and move on but this ploy did not succeed.

'We are in urgent need to locate a gallery of art,' the woman said in half broken English.

'Ja. Ja. My wife explain first to you... we must find this gallery... the address I look for on my phone.'

They spoke in German to each other for what

seemed to Oisin to be a somewhat animated and lengthy conversation. Usually of phlegmatic character, Oisin found he was beginning to feel annoyed as the two strangers did not appear to want to move away in a hurry, and although Oisin had no great plans for the morning, he just wanted to be left alone to work things out. He had no idea how to direct two confused Germans to an unknown art gallery. After, what seemed to be an hour of time, although in truth it was only five minutes, the German bellowed again. His voice was so loud that people hurrying past, looked up. Some giggled and a young man with a red beard and wearing a kilt gave the thumbs-up to Oisin.

All this began to make Oisin feel even more irritated. After all, he had no idea what the couple were talking about or why they appeared to be so agitated about finding a random art gallery.

'I really can't help you,' he said and edged sideways.

The couple moved in the same direction as if they were joined together. If Oisin hadn't been so irritated with the whole episode, it did have its amusing side. Just as he was wondering what he could do next to extricate himself from the Germans, the burly man stabbed his index finger onto Oisin's chest and exclaimed in English,

'Danke, danke. I locate the gallery of art.'

164

He bowed slightly, said something in German to his wife and the two of them headed off across a busy Princes Street without looking either left or right and leaving a slightly bemused Oisin free to wander once more.

He was grateful to sit down on a bench in the Gardens and contemplate his next move. Concerned about his sister, Mary and her whereabouts, he had no idea what to do next. He dialled her number on his phone and a voice mail message was the reply. She obviously had her phone off. This was another source of irritation for him on what was turning out to be a frustrating morning.

Although his relationship with Mary had been somewhat volcanic of late, he did feel a certain brotherly protectiveness towards her. Mary had turned into something of a puzzle and added to that her insistence that she join him in Edinburgh for whatever reason was another source of concern. She had been furtive, non-committal and totally annoying all at the same time. Oisin decided that the best course of action at the present moment was to leave things as they were and hope that Mary was back at the B and B when he returned later that day.

With that reassuring thought, he left the Gardens and crossed Princes Street. It was almost as if his feet had taken control of his mind for he found himself following in the footsteps of the annoying Germans and walking along Dundas Street past the many art galleries. It was a leisurely stroll and, with time on his hands, he peered into gallery windows, not expecting to enter any of the premises. He was attracted to one gallery where a huge painting hung filling most of the window space. The canvas was covered with vibrant blues, yellows and black. An image in the centre of the painting looked something like a winged horse, or could it be nothing more than a blob of paint splattered there to intrigue the unsuspecting observer? Did modern art have to have an existential meaning? Oisin was about to say something to that effect to another man about his own age who was studying the painting and who looked just as puzzled when from inside the gallery he heard the unmistakable boom of the German's voice.

Curiosity is a powerful trigger. It has uncovered riches, taken us to the Moon, solved many a human dilemma and then again sometimes it manifests itself as nothing more than pure and simple nosiness. After all, hasn't everyone wondered what their neighbours are doing? Oisin Kelly, with no particular purpose in mind decided to enter the art gallery and satisfy that innate curiosity. Although the Germans had annoyed him, their insistence about finding a particular gallery had intrigued him.

He thought if he just studied the paintings and other art work in the gallery as an observer, he could melt into the surroundings with little fuss, and he might find out what it was all about, that is if he kept his good ear within hearing distance of the Germans. He was amused thinking about his plan. In Edinburgh for a brief holiday and seeking out old acquaintances before going back to Kilgoolga, what harm could be done with a little snooping?

The burly German and his diminutive wife had positioned themselves in front of a huge bronze statue. Both looked furious and there was much gesturing and pointing of fingers towards a tall young man who was obviously in charge of proceedings.

'A mistake! This sculpture must not be sold. I am instructed by my employer, the Deutsche Bank, to purchase this. An email sends last week...'

'I am sorry, sir but the bronze is sold. The monies have been transferred to our account and arrangements are being made as we speak for the buyer in question to arrange delivery.'

'Nein, nein. Not acceptable. I demand to see Mr Le Bon. Now!'

The young man shrugged his shoulders and left the room. The two Germans started a very agitated conversation, none of which Oisin could understand. He hovered around carefully pretending to study paintings by the same artist whose large canvas had been on show in the window. Francesa Fitzwilliams was the name and Oisin, although not particularly enamoured with her window painting, began to admire some of her work. There's a bit of talent there, he decided and wondered if his daughter might like a painting as a gift on his return. His daughter, Suze, was the artistic one in the family.

The Germans were so engaged in their own conversation that they did not recognise Oisin as the man from whom they had asked for directions just an hour earlier. He decided it best to leave that particular re-introduction alone. He was about to leave the gallery when the tall man reappeared with another man. This man in contrast to the taller one was short and stocky with a goatee beard and grey hair. His appearance suggested that he perhaps was Mr Le Bon? Oisin decided to stay and hear what it was all about. After all, he reasoned it was good entertainment at no cost to himself.

'Good morning,' the short, stocky man said as he held out his hand in greeting. 'I am Mr Le Bon. How may I help you?'

Neither the man nor the woman extended the same courtesy. Instead, the gesture seemed to annoy both Germans.

'Why has this bronze sold? I demand an answer.

At once.'

'There has been some misunderstanding, I believe. This particular sculpture has sold. I regret if you were not informed in time. The sale has been agreed by both myself and the purchaser and is legally binding. However, I can assure you that the sculptor might be interested in creating another one... similar... and perhaps more to your liking?'

'That is not the point. I inform you on behalf of the Deutsche Bank by email that they want to purchase this particular bronze, not another one. The email was sent in good faith.'

At this point, the tall man intervened.

'I can only apologise to you, sir, but I assure you that the gallery did not receive any email from your bank regarding this particular bronze,' he said.

'Not acceptable. As you are aware, Mr Le Bon, the bank purchases work from your galleries. Perhaps we end this now.'

The exchange between the two men had turned somewhat acerbic. Anton Le Bon did not take kindly to threats. Oisin, hovering close by and trying his best not to appear to be taking much notice of what was going on, sensed the rising tension in the air. Of late he had become used to the emotional upheavals of his sister, Mary so you could say that he was finely tuned into tension.

'I regret that this is your stand on this matter,'

hissed Anton. 'But as I told you the bronze is sold. The sale has been agreed. Monies have been paid. I have offered to contact the sculptor on your behalf to commission another similar bronze if you, as a representative from the Deutsche Bank, would agree. As a gesture of goodwill I will waive the commission fee.'

The face of Anton Le Bon had turned to a bright red and Oisin noticed that both his hands were clenched into fists. He wondered if the redoubtable Mr Le Bon whose name appeared everywhere in the gallery would come to blows with the rather bad tempered German. This surely would be cause for some excitement. Oisin decided he would just wait and see what happened next. A few more people had entered the gallery and were looking in the direction of the two men and the disputed bronze.

'I need to telephone the bank now,' growled the German.

'Of course. Come into my office and you can phone from there in private.'

Anton Le Bon, his hands still clenched, marched the German and his tiny wife to his office. She scuttled behind the two men in the manner of a bantam hen fleeing a predator. The tense situation of a few seconds before seemed to have thawed. At least that's what the young man at the desk appeared to think because he gave Oisin a rather lopsided grin and walked over to him. Oisin had decided that it was about time to leave but before he did so he thought he would take a look at the disputed bronze so the two men were now face to face.

'Well, that was a close shave. Thought the two of them might come to blows. Mr Le Bon doesn't like to be challenged like that.' It was the tall young man who spoke first.

'Couldn't help but overhear,' replied Oisin. 'Don't think ye can sell it twice, do you?'

The young man laughed.

'Nay,' he said. 'Between ourselves, be glad to see the back of it. *Promy* and *Ernie the Eagle* I call it. Sat here for years. People will wonder what's become of it. See how they've rubbed the bronze on the chain. Been quite an attraction in the gallery but Mr Le Bon will replace it. He knows how to find the best sculptures around.'

Oisin, having spent time looking at all the paintings in the gallery, now turned his attention to the sculpture. It certainly was a statement piece but rather exaggerated, he decided. All of a sudden Oisin Kelly had become something of an art critic because he nodded his head and said,

'I think I have to agree with ye there. Sure like the name you have given it. Wonder what sort of space would be needed to house it though?'

'Money talks. The countess, she's the one whose bought it, must be loaded and the Deutsche Bank, well... ?' He grinned.

'I don't know much about art,' Oisin said. 'But I know what I like.'

'And *Promy and Ernie* aren't one?'

'Ye could say that. Too ostentatious for my liking.'

The tall man chuckled. He wasn't quite the entrepreneur of his employer but he could gauge whether a customer was about to buy, or not. He decided that this Irishman might just be in the market for a sale.

'Perhaps the paintings by our young artist, Francesca Fitzwilliam might be more to your taste then?' he said. 'She has talent and youth on her side. She has an unusual way with the brushwork, don't you think?'

'Aye. I've been admiring the one over there,' answered Oisin and he and the tall man studied the painting in question.

The brushwork was confidently executed. Here was an artist who wasn't afraid to experiment with colour and texture. The same winged horse as the one in the window was present but this image was fleeting, ethereal, almost hidden from view. There was much in the painting that was a joy to the senses. It was as if the artist was playing with her palette. Oisin thought it was the sort of work that you could study for hours and still find more to admire. He was tempted to buy it. He was usually of a cautious nature as far as money was concerned, having never had an overabundance of it, but there was something about this particular painting that captured his imagination. As surreal as it seemed, the painting seemed to reach out to him and almost beg him to take it.

'I'll buy it,' he said.

The tall man smiled.

'I can assure you that this will be a good investment. Mr Le Bon never takes an artist into his stable if he is unsure that monies cannot be made. Francesca has talent. Her recent one-woman exhibition was a great success for herself and for the gallery. This painting and the one in the window were the only two that didn't sell then so we decided to offer them for sale at a slightly reduced price. You can expect this painting to increase in value over the years if I'm not mistaken. Francesca is an up and coming genius.'

'I'm not buying it as an investment. I like the painting and I will hang it on my wall when I return to Australia.'

'Of course, sir. Cash or card?'

The tall man carefully wrapped the small painting in bubble pack and brown paper. He was a meticulous sort of chap, thought Oisin. The painting was then secured inside an expensive looking gold carrier bag with *Le Bon* advertised in embossed italic stripes in black. When the purchase was completed, the tall man handed Oisin the bag and his card. Oisin glanced at the name – Martin MacDonald, Art Gallery Director.

The two men shook hands.

'I hope you have a safe trip back to Australia and if we can be of any other service to you, Mr Kelly...?'

Oisin, happy with his unexpected purchase, grinned,

'Thanks, mate,' he said. 'I'll be off soon down under but I've a few things to do before then. For sure I'll be tellin' people about your gallery. The name of *Le Bon* will travel with me to the other side of the earth...'

'We have a gallery in Melbourne, by the way.' Martin MacDonald replied.

'Well, ye never know. Maybe I'll visit that one someday and buy another painting. Life throws up some surprises, doesn't it now?'

'It sure does, Mr Kelly. It sure does.'

That was the end of the transaction between the two men as Martin turned his attention to his laptop and began to punch in the keys leaving Oisin a much happier man than he had been before he entered the gallery.

As he made to leave with the Francesca Fitzwilliam painting, Mr Le Bon and the two Germans appeared. Mr Le Bon said something to his gallery director who nodded his head in what seemed to Oisin to be an agreement. When Mr Le Bon offered his hand to the German the gesture wasn't reciprocated. Instead, the German clicked his heels, took his wife's arm, brushed rather rudely against Oisin and the two of them left the gallery. Oisin heard Mr Le Bon mutter something to the effect that that was the end of it.

'Here's the contact to ring at the Deutsche Bank, Martin,' he said. 'We'll not see those two again.'

And Mr Le Bon turned and walked back towards his office leaving Oisin thinking what an interesting morning he had had and what a surprise it was for him to have bought a painting on impulse. Maybe Mary, the artist might be interested? Surely this might be a way of communicating with his sister on her level. With this optimistic thought, Oisin headed back towards Princes Street and the crowds.

****

Oisin was surprised to find Mary at the B and B and for once she appeared pleased to see him. This was unexpected as she had been somewhat elusive since their arrival in Edinburgh. He had tried without success to contact her by phone and text during the day. Now positioned on one of the lounge chairs in a somewhat casual pose with both her legs resting on the armrest and her shoes off, she was reading a magazine when he entered the room. It looked as if she intended to settle down and make herself at home with no thought of propriety to the B and B owner who was nowhere to be seen. When she saw him, she cried out,

'Where have you been, Oisin? I've been lookin' for you all day.'

'I tried to call ye. No answer.'

'Well, so you say.' Mary pouted.

'Oh, for feck's sake, Mary. Give it a rest.'

An uneasy silence followed. Oisin sat down on the other armchair and rested the painting on his knee.

'What's that?' Mary asked and she pointed to the painting that had been wrapped up so very neatly by Martin MacDonald at the gallery.

'Oh... something that might be of interest to ye.'

'Show me then?' She was like a child, eager and excited all at once. Mary was like that, Oisin thought. She could swing from one mood to the next in a split second. He hesitated for a moment before replying. He was never sure of Mary's reactions these days. Seeing a painting by an unknown artist might annoy her or it might inspire her. You never knew.

'I've had quite a day,' he said.

'Doing what?'

'Oh, this and that. I walked into town and down Dundas Street.'

'Where the galleries are?'

'Aye.'

'Well, what's in the bag then? Don't be so mysterious.'

Oisin carefully opened the wrapping and the Francesa Fitzwilliam painting came into view. He held it up on his knee so Mary could study it from a distance. No one spoke. A few minutes later a highly ornate and colourful cuckoo clock on the wall opposite Oisin broke the silence as the mechanism and the bird announced the time to be six o'clock. The clock had been under discussion that morning for hadn't the B and B owner regaled Oisin with the story of how she had bought it in Switzerland and what difficulty she had had convincing the Customs Officer that it hadn't been filled with drugs? The mere idea of the rather severe looking B and B lady being a drug runner had slightly amused Oisin but he listened to her long winded story with at least the appearance of some interest.

Mary leaped from her chair in one surprising agile movement for one who was well into her fifties and clapped her hands.

'Oisin, where did you get this? Don't tell me you bought it, ye old skinflint.'

'That I did,' replied Oisin. 'Now, Mary, ye being an artist an' all, what do ye think of it?'

'Genius.' Mary studied the painting with an artist's eye before replying, 'Whoever did this knows how to apply colour. Look at the way the swirl of blue and black brings the winged horse alive. Can ye see it there?' And she pointed to a particularly bright patch of paint in the centre of the painting. Oisin, having studied the painting in the gallery for a good half hour had indeed not noticed Mary's keen observation.

'Aye, I see it now,' he said. 'I just liked the painting,' he added pleased that his sister had shown such enthusiasm for his purchase. 'I was told the artist is an up and coming young lady... Francesca Fitzwilliam... have ye heard of her?'

'Can't say I have.'

Brother and sister sat in silence, both studying the painting that by some miracle appeared to have brought the two of them closer, if just for a few minutes.

It was then that Mary noticed the designer carrier bag that had held the painting. She picked it up and frowned.

'Where... where did ye buy the painting, Oisin?'

'Oh. I happened to wander into a gallery after I met two Germans earlier. They asked me for directions in Princes Street and I sort of saw them again in the gallery.'

'I'm not interested in any Germans, Oisin,' Mary hissed.

'Oh, well. It was *Le Bon,* an upmarket sort of place I believe. So up market that there's no need to add the word gallery, least that's what I was told.'

'Le Bon.'

'Aye.'

'Anton.'

'Aye, that's right. Anton Le Bon.'

If he had been more observant, Oisin would have noticed that Mary had turned around so as not to look at him and that her usual bright cheeks were now pale under her makeup.

CHAPTER NINE

A chance remark? A chance encounter? Is there ever such a thing as pure chance? Destiny plays tricks and the unexpected remark can sometimes lead us down a different path from the one we thought we were travelling. So it was when Mary Kelly heard her brother say that distant but often remembered name, and with barely a shrug of his shoulders, not perceiving that the tension in the room had gone up a notch after the mention of that particular name, he would have been surprised beyond words. But Oisin hadn't noticed any of the change in Mary and if he had, he would have put it down to her mental condition, a malady that controlled her moods and something that he was still in the process of coming to terms with. No, Oisin would not have believed in a million years that the gallery owner whom he had seen so briefly would have been known to his sister and the mere mention of his name would have caused such a change in her whole demeanour.

'Let me look at the painting, Oisin. I want to study it,' Mary had regained something of her composure. Something within her wanted to investigate this work by the unknown artist, this Francesca Fitzwilliam, the latest prodigy of Anton Le Bon. Memories and so much that was unresolved came into her thoughts at that moment. If Oisin could have read her mind, he would have stormed out of the house to confront Anton Le Bon. He might have even come to blows with the gallery owner, or at the very least gave him a piece of his mind in no uncertain words, such is the bond that often exists between siblings when one of them is threatened.

Oisin handed the painting almost reverently to his sister. She was able to balance this particular work of art on her knee for it was small in comparison to the other paintings that usually adorned the walls of the Le Bon gallery. Anton always had an eye for talent for hadn't she been one of his recent discoveries? He would flatter the young Francesca Fitzwilliam with a promise of riches and fame, Mary could almost hear his voice in her ear as she studied the fine work by this young woman. What strange quirk had made her usually non-artistic brother be drawn to this particular painting and why had he purchased it? Size, in this case would matter. Oisin could not afford the high prices of the larger paintings in the Le Bon gallery of that she was certain.

'There's talent there to be sure,' she said to Oisin after a few moments.

'Aye. Right enough. Can't quite figure it out but I like it. My daughter is quite an artist, Mary. I bought if for her but I'll enjoy looking at it before she sees it and then, what a story for her. Her father buying a painting in Edinburgh, now that's a thought.' Oisin chuckled. 'I'm no artist, Mary, but I knew I just had to buy this. It was a totally weird experience. The winged horse seemed to leap out at me and at that moment, I couldn't think of anything else except I wanted it. Strange, don't ye think?'

Mary did not answer.

****

When Mary heard Oisin say the name Anton Le Bon, her first thought was that this was some sort of cruel joke Fate had played upon her. In her mind, Anton Le Bon was the only reason she Edinburgh and having Oisin by her side was the perfect excuse to be there. Over the years, she followed the art dealer's progress in the art world and jealously hated him for everything. The monetary wealth he had appeared to have acquired through his sometimes shady dealings was just one of the many things that gnawed at the heart of Mary. There was no doubt that Anton was a ruthless exploiter of other people's talent for hadn't she once been under his spell just as she imagined the young artist, Francesca Fitzwilliam would be now. Sleep did not come to her that night. She tossed and turned and tried not to think but that was an impossible situation and in the end she gave up. She dressed hurriedly, pulling on a waterproof coat and sturdy walking boots and left the B and B about five o'clock in the morning before the city was awake.

She walked at a brisk pace along the street, looking neither to the left nor to the right except to glance once in the direction of Arthur's Seat, that unmistakable and much loved volcanic hill which somehow defined Edinburgh. The hill was now covered in a fine mist. Early morning joggers like black and distant dots on the hill were the only signs of life. That other iconic symbol of the city, Edinburgh Castle was hidden behind an even darker shroud of mist. Mary quickened her pace. She wondered whether should she join the joggers on the hill and hope that the fresh morning air would give her time to think as to her next move. Her thoughts were like butterflies, flitting from one thing to the next but it was Anton Le Bon and his galleries that kept coming into her mind most of the time. She was angry with herself for these thoughts were akin to some sort of cancer that wouldn't go away. But then, she often thought of Anton.

She turned towards the Centenary Pool and it was here that she encountered an old woman of about eighty, bent down by age and dragging what looked like an overloaded shopping trolley behind her. She stopped in front of Mary and blocked her path. Mary, her thoughts on Anton, nearly collided with her and in thus doing came face to face with the old woman. This was quite an achievement considering there was no one else about.

'Hello, dearie, can you spare a few pennies for me? I'm fair parched for a cup o' tea.'

Mary had no sympathy in her soul for those less fortunate than herself. She viewed beggars as scum and if she had her way they would all be banished out of sight, out of mind. This was somewhat surprising as Mary herself had once been in a similar position after Anton tired of her but then, it is often by seeing our faults mirrored in others that bring to mind our own failings. Mary had blocked all memory of being homeless and on the streets. That experience had in fact just lasted a day or two, and it had happened many years ago, and the memory of it was almost forgotten. Angry now with this unfortunate woman who looked as if she hadn't washed herself for days, her breath as foul as any down town bar and with two front teeth missing, Mary's instinct was to push the intruder out of the way by force if necessary. This creature had not been homeless for days. In fact, by her appearance she had survived on the streets for years and here she was, tattered, filthy and old and begging for a cup of tea.

'Get out of my way,' Mary hissed.

The old woman took no heed of Mary's words. Instead, she laid a filthy hand onto Mary's. Her face was now inches away. Mary caught a whiff of foul breath. The old woman's eyes were pale blue, watery, and desperate. Whispers of grey hair were visible under a red woollen beret. A black and blue tartan scarf, torn at both ends and tucked loosely around her neck completed the sorry picture. Her grubby tweed overcoat had seen better days. Frayed at the sleeves the coat somehow looked out of place and appeared to be a few sizes too large for this pitiful stranger. It covered a feeble and forlorn figure. All this further gave the appearance of one who was really 'down on their luck.'

'Could ye no spare me somethin', dearie? I'll no trouble you again but it's a hard thing to be gettin' old an' nothin' to eat.'

The woman's persistence further frustrated Mary. There was money in her pocket but her heart was as cold as the old woman's hand which now had tightened its grip around her arm. The proximity, the smell and the feeling that this stranger was invading both her space and her safety further angered an already irritated Mary.

'I've no money to give to the likes of you.'

The old woman didn't answer. Instead, she pushed her face even closer towards Mary. The sadness in her eyes was so plain to see that Mary stepped backward to avoid being in such close proximity to another's misery. For ever such a brief moment, Mary even felt pity for this uninvited stranger. It was a short-lived, however, because a young man of about thirty called out,

'Hiya, Doris. What ya up to today?'

The young man bounced towards the old woman and Mary in the manner of a large energetic Great Dane dog. He was tall, red haired, with a freckled face and muscular arms and legs. Although there was still a spring chill in the air, he wore a light shirt, shorts and trainers and he carried a carrier bag with a towel flung over one shoulder. He was obviously bound for the swimming pool. When the old woman saw him, a slight smile appeared and she released her grip on Mary's arm.

'Why, hello, Pete,' she replied. 'I'm on my way to the Balmoral for my breakfast.'

'Och, awa' wi' ye, Doris. Here's somethin' for a bacon buttie at the chippie.' And he pressed a five pound note into her outstretched and eager hand.

'I am off then to partake of some early morning refreshments. My thanks, young man.'

'Nae worries, Doris. See ye around.'

Doris turned her back on both Mary and the young man and, dragging her trolley behind her, set off in the direction of the main thoroughfare where no doubt, she would partake of a suitable breakfast, but definitely not at the iconic Balmoral.

'That was generous of you,' said Mary to the young man.

'It's nothin'. Fond of the old Doris. Do ye ken who she is?'

'A bag lady.'

The young man laughed.

'She is now but she's one of the McMahons. Ye ken.'

'Never heard of them.'

'Och, well. They're filthy rich. Think Doris was one of five girls. They've a place out Morningside way and a castle somewhere in the Highlands. Cannae remember just where offhand. Made their fortune wi' the slave trade, ye ken, had plantations in the Caribbean. Now, they just live on the earnings from the backs of others.'

'I find it hard to believe. She's an old tramp.'

'Ye never ken, de ye naw? Doris was the rebel. Ran off with a black man, think he was a musician, family disowned her. Don't know what happened to the man but Doris never went back to her family. She's an Embra institution now. I like to give her a quid or two now and then. She's a harmless old biddie.'

Mary was silent. The whole episode had annoyed her and she just wanted to get away but then, whenever there was a crisis, Mary always wanted to 'get away.'

A few seconds later and the young man had bounded up the steps to the pool, three at a time. She could hear him whistling to himself as he entered the building.

****

That morning Oisin looked again for his sister, Mary. He knocked on her door but all was quiet. Puzzled, he sat down at the breakfast table and waited for the B and B owner to arrive. She did a moment or two later and this time, she was even more talkative. Given that Oisin and Mary had now spent a few nights with her as paying guests, there was a familiar tone to her greeting.

'Good morning to ye, Oisin,' she announced. 'And what would ye by havin' today?'

'Full Scottish.'

The B and B owner nodded with appreciation. She liked her guests to enjoy a hearty breakfast although these days there seemed to be a lot of fussy eaters around with all manner of food preferences. At least, this Irishman did not fit into that category. He wiped his plate clean, ate every piece of toast with lashings of butter, and drained the teapot. When she returned with a generous bowl of porridge, Oisin said,

'Has my sister been down for breakfast?'

'Aye. Just a slice of toast and marmalade an' a cup of tea, she had. Eats like a sparrow, that one. An' aff she went. Not a word as to where. Reckon she might 'ave a fancy man around the place. Better watch oot.' Her usual severe manner betrayed the slightest possibility of a grin.

'I doubt that,' answered Oisin but he was worried. What on earth was Mary up to?

****

The city woke. Now Mary had to compete with space with workers and students as she made her way across the Royal Mile towards Princes Street. At the Balmoral Hotel, a gaudy American wearing a tartan beret and sporting an equally flamboyant tartan scarf blocked her path.

'Why, hi de, Ma'am,' he bellowed. 'Ain't this just the finest of cities? Why, my ancestors came from this here Edinburgh, you know. Don't you just love the place? Right proud of my Scots roots, ain't that just so, Muriel?' He looked to the woman beside him for verification and she nodded just as enthusiastically. She was dressed as gaudily as her husband with a tartan beret and scarf to match.

'That's a sure thing. My folks came from

Ireland, from County Cork, ya know. I just love it over here. It's so small not like the States, is it Herbert?'

'And ain't it a fact that the people are so friendly. Well, right pleased to meet you, Ma'am,' said Herbert and he held out his hand to Mary. She took hold of it and nearly fell over, his grip was so tight.

What with the old tramp at the swimming pool and now these two annoying Americans who were intent on treating her like some long lost acquaintance, Mary could feel the anger rising up inside her. Any moment she would snap. She took a deep breath and pulled away from the American's tight grasp. He was holding her hand for longer than was necessary, and certainly this was not the behaviour of polite society. She put her head in the air and without one word, continued up Princes Street.

She walked at a brisk pace towards a group of about twenty French students. The young people were quite noisy and didn't appear to be taking much notice of their teachers. Most of them were looking at their phones and talking amongst themselves. They had spread out at the entrance to the Gardens and people had to walk onto the road to get by. By now Mary was becoming even more agitated. The behaviour of the students and their seemingly oblivious trouble they were causing to the pedestrians, further irritated her. Mary was not known for her patience and when one of the students, a thin, scrawny lad with black hair to his shoulders, pushed her as she endeavoured to get past, she spat out,

'Let me through!'

He looked up from his phone and seeing this middle aged woman with a fierce expression on her face, he shrugged his shoulders and moved back a pace. The other students near him started to giggle. Mary's schoolgirl French did not understand a word that was said around her and this further annoyed her. A moment later a path was cleared for her when the offending students shuffled away in the direction of the Floral Clock. The thin, scrawny lad did not look up from his phone but he followed his friends as if he was joined to them by a string. Now Mary was able to cross Princes Street and continue on her quest.

Ever since Oisin had shown her the painting by Francesca Fitzwilliam and she heard the name of Anton Le Bon, Mary's thoughts had been focused on one thing, and one thing alone. She had no idea if Anton would be in Edinburgh as his movements over the years were sketchy. She had followed his rise to celebrity status as his galleries increased in number, and he became known as one of the richest men around; the subject of envy and admiration in equal measure, and fawned over by the sycophants.

Whenever Mary thought of Anton, a deep, silent fury rose within her. He was her nemesis and she hated him with a loathing that at times took over her mind. When this happened, she lost all sense of reason so great was the emotion. Many times she had wished him dead and in those dark moments, she plotted the many ways to go about this grim act. Now she was within striking distance of this loathsome creature, as she had named him in her mind, and it was all thanks to her brother, Oisin who had somehow stumbled into Anton's gallery in Edinburgh.

She walked faster down Dundas Street, stopping every now and then to peer into gallery windows. She paused once beside an impressive ladies dress shop, and wondered just for a moment, whether she should venture inside. In her better days, Mary had dressed well and she still loved the feel of beautiful dresses and the sensuous pleasure wearing them did for her. Then she remembered her mission. If Oisin was right, Anton's gallery was in this street, and she was determined to see him again. He would be surprised to meet her, if indeed; he remembered what they had meant to each other all those years ago. The possibility that her nemesis might not even recognise her further ignited that silent fury within. No, she thought, Anton must pay for what he did.

She stood like a statue on the pavement, not looking to the left or the right as all those emotions swept through her once again. Just admiring the dresses in the window brought back a memory of Anton and the way he had looked at her that evening so long ago when she had dressed to please him and worn a beautiful low cut burgundy ball gown specially made for her by a talented dressmaker that Anton knew. The satin fabric and colour had been chosen by him and the dressmaker had discussed the style with him, not once consulting Mary as to her wishes. Anton had insisted that she dress appropriately for a special occasion, and he had taken her, hand in hand, to an upmarket dress shop in Kensington where the beautiful ball gown was purchased, no expense spared that day, for Anton had already began to make money and she was no longer the poor Irish girl from the west of Ireland, without guile and penniless.

It had been an evening to remember. She was nervous and spilt some of the red wine over the ball gown. The wine had gone to her head and made her slightly dizzy. Anton was annoyed after that and left her standing alone amongst the crowd of pretentious folk. Wealth, it seemed, brought little happiness to them. Their shrill voices still rang in her ears, if she thought for a moment; she could hear them even now. She knew they mocked her and there was much innuendo. Her innocence made her vulnerable to their sneers and Anton did nothing to defend her. Later, he had told her she must learn to conduct herself in high society for that was where he intended to be, and if she wished to remain in their relationship, she would need to do as he instructed. She lay beside him that night and her tears filled her eyes and left wet patches on her pillow. In the early morning, she crept out of the bed, as silently as she could so as not to awaken him, and curled up on the large armchair like some tiny, wounded animal, scared and alone.

Now, all those years later, she was once again close to Anton Le Bon and the possibility of what she should do once she confronted him weighed heavily on her mind. Revenge is bittersweet. She had rehearsed their meeting many times but now that the letters in gold above the large window came into view, *Le Bon,* her resolve weakened. The gallery was across the street from where she stood. Just a few steps away and she may once again encounter the loathing individual who was Anton Le Bon. She had waited so long for this moment.

She crossed the street to the gallery and pretended to study the large work of art in the window, *The Winged Horse,* by that up and coming new artist, Francesca Fitzwilliam, both the artist and the painting that Oisin had been so enthusiastic about, and what had been like an omen to bring her to this moment. She shivered even though the sun was warm in a cloudless blue sky. Much to her surprise, she noticed that her hands were moist. With a pounding heart and clenched fists, she opened the door to *Le Bon.*

CHAPTER TEN

When Mary entered the gallery, she was surprised at the space inside. Even with the ferocity she felt towards Anton, she had to admit that he always knew how to make a room impressive so as to attract the buyers. The art gallery in Edinburgh looked as if this was another of his success stories. What greeted her was the massive sculpture of Prometheus and the Eagle. Two workmen were in the process of attempting to move

it and this was causing them some difficulty for there was much grunting and grumbling, and the occasional expletive. A tall, thin man dressed in a grey tailored suit, and by his very appearance an employee of the gallery, was busy directing the procedure but when he noticed that a potential customer had entered the room, he stopped, said something to the workmen and approached a rather unsure Mary.

'Apologies for the inconvenience,' he said in a jovial manner. 'This fine sculpture has been sold and it has to be removed from the gallery today as the buyer is arriving later, I believe. Feel free to look around. We have some paintings by Francesca Fitzwilliam in this room and we have a mixed media exhibition by various artists here, and there's pottery, ceramic art and woodwork in the two rooms at the back. If I may be of any assistance, please ask...'

'Is Anton Le Bon here?'

The direct question caught the tall man by surprise and he hesitated before he replied.

'I don't think he is, Madam. I believe he is at a meeting at present. May I take your name..?'

The obvious dismissal of her enquiry annoyed an already anxious Mary. She didn't

answer. Instead, she turned around and walked to the entrance of the gallery without looking to the left or the right. Then, with her hand on the door handle, she said,

'Tell him someone he knew a long time ago wishes to meet him again. He'll remember... an Irishwoman of his acquaintance.'

****

Oisin Kelly had long given up the idea of coincidences in life. People had arrived unexpected when he needed them or at other crucial times he had been thinking of someone, and lo and behold they had called him or he had met them in an unexpected place. He often thought that this wasn't coincidence at all but rather that life was filled with a wonderful synchronicity if you would only allow it to happen. Life, with all its challenges, would flow in a more perfect pattern if coincidences were not viewed as something mysterious and beyond our understanding. Acceptance, he reasoned was key to a happy life and that was most evident when the so called coincidences were seen in an altogether different way. So, when he saw his sister, Mary standing outside the *Le Bon* he was pleased but not surprised. After all, he had been wandering the streets and sending her messages on his phone all morning. He reasoned that with the mysterious power of thought, she was bound to pick up his ambiances sooner or later and they would meet. What caused him to once again wander down Dundas Street was another of life's mysteries?

When he got nearer to Mary, however, he was alarmed to see that she was not at all at ease. Her face was set in that peculiar way of hers when her emotions were out of control. Many times he had been subject to this look since Ballybeg. A passing thought occurred to him that she may ignore him or even strike out the way she had done to him on the beach when they first met. Either way would be an embarrassment in the city street. He approached her with caution.

'Mary,' he said, 'I've been looking for ye, so I have. All morning... did ye get my messages?'

His sister didn't reply. A troubled Oisin thought that she wasn't going to speak to him. Mary had all the look of a stranger. This further alarmed him. What on earth had happened to her?

'Come now, Mary,' he continued. 'Ye don't look at all well, so. Why, you're tremblin' all over. What on God's earth have ye been doin' to yerself?'

But Mary didn't reply. Her eyes fixed upon his face and she shivered even though it was a warm day, and the sun was high in the sky. Now Oisin was fearful. He tried again.

'Let's sit yeself down somewhere and tell me what's happened to ye?'

He put his arm around her waist to steady her as a mother would to a child. The brother and sister then proceeded to hobble along the pavement. A few seconds later Mary stopped as if she was unable to move and the effort was too much for her. People pushed past them. Everyone was in a hurry. In this city street, their personal circumstance had become a microcosm of other people's lives. The people hurrying past them, although unaware of what was happening to these two strangers, were somehow connected to them. The mere fact of being human linked them as distress is universal. Oisin had one aim and that was to find the safety of somewhere to sit, to breathe, to recover, to understand. Here, he could try to uncover the reasons for Mary's distress.

When they reached the corner of the street, Oisin navigated Mary towards an empty park bench set in a relative secluded park with less people and just the odd city pigeons for a distraction. Then he took hold of Mary's hand. She shivered when she felt his touch and for a second he wondered if she would strike out at him once again but instead she leaned her head against his shoulder and closed her eyes. It was the closest they had been to physical contact in such a long time. She was his little sister again, needing him.

It was now lunchtime and more people arrived in the park from the offices and shops. A young man of about twenty with a head of black hair standing up in spikes thanks to a generous use of gel and both his arms decorated in tattoos, sat down beside them on their bench and, without asking permission to do so, proceeded to eat a sandwich and drink a takeaway coffee. His presence annoyed Oisin but Mary didn't appear to notice the intruder. She seemed content to be close to Oisin for once. She had been breathless when he first encountered her but now her breathing was more even and relaxed. They sat like this for about a quarter of an hour, not speaking, just watching the people and the pigeons and the odd grey squirrel.

When the spiky headed young man stood up to leave after throwing a few left over crumbs to an appreciative and vocal pigeon, Oisin asked Mary again what was wrong. She raised her head from his shoulder, frowned, and then just as abruptly she took her hand away from his. The connection between them which had been so precious a few moments before ended with that one gesture.

He was surprised at what happened next. Instead of answering his question, she rose to her feet and, without a word, turned away from him. She did not look back. With a heavy heart, he watched the retreating figure, losing sight of her when she joined the small crowd waiting for the lights to change at the corner of the street.

****

Life at *Le Bon* was hectic. This was the day that the Countess di Laguna had informed the ever efficient Martin MacDonald by email that she would be arriving to oversee the transportation of *Promy and Ernie the Eagle* to Italy; not that she was aware of Marin's pet name for the sculpture in question and even if she knew, it would have amused her more than offended her for the countess, in her wisdom, had decided that it was time for her to visit Edinburgh and surprise Anton Le Bon. The sculpture it has to be said did intrigue her when she first viewed it online. It would make an impressive feature for her husband to drool over; the count who was an admirer of the male body and the image of a man wrestling an eagle would appeal to his masculine instincts. The count liked beautiful things and their marriage had seen all manner of beautiful things, the steady stream of Adonis looking young men who turned up at their villa, just the human side of his need for possessions. Fine wines and beautiful things were the Count di Laguna's passion. His wife, the beautiful Sophia Caputo fitted into his world as neatly as a silken glove. Their marriage had survived and blossomed along with all his other beautiful things. Theirs was a convenient arrangement based on appearance and social standing. They loved each other in a comfortable way, both aware of the need to pursue their separate paths. Neither ever considered the need to part company from each other. When Sophia gave birth to their daughter, Isabella, the count decided his duty was done. They were never lovers in the traditional way but they were definitely kindred spirits and friends for life. The count would be delighted with the purchase of Prometheus and the Eagle.

Martin MacDonald knew at once that the grey haired woman who entered the gallery was the Countess di Laguna. By the way she glided into the room with head held high; this had to be the buyer of the much maligned sculpture. He shook her hand and rather wished at that moment that he could have responded in an altogether Italian way, and kissed that hand. The countess had that effect on men. He introduced himself as the Art Gallery Director and what a pleasure it was to meet the purchaser of this impressive work of art, such a unique sculpture that would be perfect in the right setting. The bronze had been subject to much interest, why earlier a German buyer had been most upset that it had been sold.

The countess nodded her head in approval. The bronze was a gift to her husband, the count, she said. He knew nothing of its purchase and would be overjoyed to possess it. A few years ago the count and she had met the sculptor at their villa in Bologna and the sculptor had informed them there that he was in the process of working on a bronze from Greek mythology as he was captivated by the male figure. The story of Prometheus had intrigued him since he had been a boy. In fact, as he worked he became even more inspired and the whole project was a joy for him. The count had been most enthusiastic when he heard that. It was Fate that the countess had been browsing online and discovered that the famous *Le Bon* had acquired the sculpture in question. It was too good an opportunity to miss, and she had decided then and there to travel to Edinburgh to view Prometheus and the Eagle in situ before shipping it to Italy, she would like to assure herself that the sculpture was as described, and perhaps meet the owner of the gallery, Anton Le Bon?

'Certainly,' replied the now somewhat flustered Martin MacDonald, 'Our workmen have packaged the sculpture securely and all arrangements are in place for shipment. Please come with me.'

The countess followed Martin to a room at the back of the gallery where she discovered that *Prometheus and the Eagle* were as described safely secured in packaging material, ready to go. The countess examined the sculpture as best she could despite the fact that it was covered in layers of plastic wrapping. She nodded her head in approval.

'I wish now to meet with Mr Le Bon.'

'Of course, countess,' replied Martin somewhat surprised by the request. 'I will see if Mr Le Bon is available. He was at a meeting earlier but I am sure he would like to meet Prometheus's buyer. The sculpture has been here a while and we have become quite fond of it, it has to be said.'

The last few words of the conversation were added without a flicker of emotion.

Back at his desk, Martin spoke through the intercom to his employer.

'Countess di Laguna is here to view Prometheus,' he said in a somewhat hushed voice. 'She would like to meet you if that is at all possible,

Mr Le Bon.'

Turning to the countess, he said that Mr Le Bon was indeed available and that he would welcome an opportunity to meet with the buyer of the famous sculpture.

A few minutes later, Anton emerged from his office with a smile on his face.

'Countess di Laguna,' he said. 'It's a pleasure to meet with you.'

Much to Martin MacDonald's astonishment, Anton Le Bon inclined his head, and then without a moment's hesitation, kissed the hand of the countess before escorting her to his office where he shut the door firmly behind them both.

****

When Anton Le Bon heard that Sophia di Laguna would be paying him a visit in Edinburgh, the first thing he did was end the relationship with his University lecturer in Molecular Chemistry. This was done amicably enough. After all, they were both adults and neither had expected their affair to last longer than six months. It had surprised them both that they had been together now, off and on for nearly two years. Neither had much to say to each other after the sex act anyhow.

The next thing that Anton did was to rent a

cottage on one of the Outer Hebridean islands where he planned to spend time with his beloved Sophia, away from prying eyes and the inevitable gossip which would certainly be the case if they had stayed in Edinburgh; discretion being the order of the day. Although Anton was well known for his numerous affairs and the aging Lothario was subject to some amusement in certain bar room conversations, his long term relationship with the Italian countess was a well-kept secret. He had only truly loved one woman and that woman was the Countess di Laguna, his Sophia. To expose that love now after all these years would be a foolhardy thing to do in his opinion and one he would never contemplate doing no matter what happened. To everyone he met, Sophia was to be introduced as the countess who had come to Edinburgh to purchase the famous bronze statue for her husband, Count Alexandro di Laguna. In public they would appear as acquaintances, not lovers. For that reason, the week on the remote island could be arranged without anyone suspecting anything. Everyone would think that the bronze had been be shipped back to Italy along with the countess and Anton could inform his staff at the gallery that he had business elsewhere and was not be contacted under any circumstances. As he was often away from his Edinburgh gallery this should not pose a problem.

He and Sophia would slip out of Edinburgh in his BMW, take the ferry to the island and enjoy seven glorious days of tranquillity. This was his plan. He did not reckon on the eagle eye of his gallery director for Martin MacDonald had noticed the unexpected signs of intimacy that had occurred between his employer and the Italian buyer of Prometheus. Over the years Martin had learned to be discreet and turn a blind eye to the number of women, who to all intents and purposes had become Anton's latest lovers, but this Italian woman was not the same somehow. Anton acted differently around her.

For Martin there was also the problem of the strange woman he thought was Irish who had turned up asking to see Anton. In the rush to get the bronze ready for shipment before the countess arrived, Martin had completely forgotten to mention the Irishwoman. It was only after all the excitement had died down and the countess had been escorted to the door of the gallery by an attentive Anton that Martin remembered.

'I meant to say, Anton,' said Martin for the two men were on first name terms when no one was about, 'I forgot to mention that someone was asking for you.'

'Oh?'

'Aye, didn't give her name. Thought she was

acting a bit odd, if you ask me. Came into the gallery with a look on her face and didn't want to see anything, just wanted to meet you. When I said you weren't available, she got angry, I thought. Then she didn't say another word except something about you knowing her a long time ago. A bit of a nutter if you ask me.'

A frown appeared on Anton's brow followed by a puzzled look.

'You say an Irishwoman?'

'Aye.'

'How old do you think she was?'

'No spring chicken that's for sure. In her fifties, I guess. As I said, she was just here for a few minutes and then she disappeared out the door.'

'Well, I've met a lot of Irishwomen... and men... in my life, Martin. Can't be expected to remember them all.'

'Right enough. I'm the same. Must try to remember names. People like to think you know their name but this woman didn't give her name, so guess it wasn't that important.'

'You're probably right, Martin,' replied Anton but he still had a frown on his face.

****

Oisin was surprised to find Mary back at the B and

B when he returned later that day. She was pleased to see him and now wore a floral skirt to her ankles and a white blouse, a string of colourful beads around her neck and large circular silver earrings. In fact, her whole appearance had changed with a liberal amount of face powder and eye makeup. She had taken care applying it and looked completely different with a bright red lipstick on her lips. Normally she wore no makeup. This was a changed Mary from the one he had tried to pacify earlier in the day.

'Let's go out for a meal, Oisin,' she said when she saw him. 'My treat.'

Ever willing to agree to anything that approached normalcy with his sister, Oisin nodded his head in approval.

'Why not?'

They found a delightful Italian restaurant hidden away from the tourist traffic. Here brother and sister enjoyed a pizza and a bottle of red wine. Mary was more relaxed than she had been in a long time, perhaps helped by the amount of wine she drank. She was an engaging conservationist and talked freely on a range of subjects.

Their conversation inevitably got round to art. When she asked him what had attracted him to the Fitzwilliam painting, he was at a loss for words. Rather lamely he told her that he had just liked it.

She laughed then. Mary rarely laughed. In fact, in the weeks that he had been with her, this was the first time he felt that she had reverted back to the carefree sister he had known in his youth.

She took another sip of wine.

'We dined out a lot you know, Oisin,' she said. 'When I lived in London.'

'The good life,' he said.

'Sometimes, not always.'

She frowned. Her moods could change in an instant.

'What made you go to that gallery... *Le Bon?*'

'Thought we were talkin' about pizzas and dining out.'

She shrugged her shoulders.

'Well, why did you?'

'Did what?'

'Go to that gallery and buy the painting.'

'Oh, long story. I told ye I had these two Germans wantin' directions to a gallery in Dundas Street and then I saw them again in *Le Bon*... nothing better to do, and I just walked in.'

'Did you see Anton?'

'Anton?'

'Where ye bought the painting that you were so on about.'

'Who are ye talkin' about, Mary? Who is this Anton?'

'Anton Le Bon.'

'The gallery owner?'

'Aye. The gallery owner.'

'There was a short, stubby character there I think. Seemed to be the boss. I just met the gallery manager... Martin MacDonald I think his name was... ye know what I'm like with names but I can't remember meeting an Anton.'

'You would remember him if you met him,' and she glared at Oisin.

He was puzzled now, and he said, 'How do ye know this Anton fella?'

'I knew him a long time ago.'

She stood up and gulped down the last remaining drop of wine in her glass.

'Guess if ye were both in the art world in London... ?' he asked naively.

'I knew him, Oisin,' she replied. 'I knew him and I have come to Edinburgh for one reason.'

'Thought it was because of me?' Oisin joked.

Mary didn't reply. It was when they were out in the street that she answered him.

'Do you want to know the reason?'

'Aye. Don't leave me in suspense, sister dear.'

'I am going to kill Anton Le Bon,' she said.

PART THREE

RESOLUTION

CHAPTER ELEVEN

One of the reasons Oisin wanted to see Edinburgh again before he left for Australia was a simple one but one he kept to himself, not trusting his family to know his motives, although he guessed they wouldn't have much interest anyway. What was past was past, and not one of them had ever questioned as to why he so abruptly left Edinburgh all those years ago, not saying a word, not even to his mother, left, and disappeared to the other side of the earth. Years later Frankie managed to track him down in Kilgoolga but when the brothers met so much had gone under the bridge, so to speak, that that particular subject wasn't mentioned. Oisin, haunted by Cecy and eager to impress his elder brother had no wish to discuss the reasons then, or now. The love affair with Cecy was a bitter sweet memory, at the back of his mind, but ever present there nevertheless, and all tied up with his rapid departure from Edinburgh. The move turned out to be a positive one. Against all the odds, he made a go of it as the Aussies told him on many occasions. Living in that vast expanse of a country and marrying a local girl had made all the difference, then and now. If he had remained in Edinburgh every street corner and every park bench would hold the memory of Cecy.

Nostalgia can play tricks on the mind. This was surely the case with Oisin for the remembrance of his youth that he treasured the most in so many ways, and what he perceived, forty years later to be happier and freer days in that Edinburgh was all tied up with the family he met there, not Cecy. He had been an innocent abroad with the American Cecy. Not so, with the Italian family, the Luchettas. Meeting Silvio, his sister, Rosa Cavellessi and the rest of the family in the agreeable setting of 42 Willow Crescent had proved just what was needed at that time for the young Irishman. It was his dying Uncle Mick who sent him on a mission to Edinburgh. It was there that more revelations about Mick, Rosa and their daughter, Concetta had been revealed to the naïve Oisin but as it turned out, a pleasant one. Oisin and Concetta had become friends. Now, the urge to become reunited with the family of his memory was paramount in his mind. But then, 42 Willow Crescent might not be there? And the Luchetta family, would they recognise an older Oisin, grey haired and deaf in one ear? Silvio and Rosa would have to be dead and Concetta? Then there was her older sister, Silvio's daughter, Isabella, what would have become of her? It was all a gamble.

But Mary's shock announcement that she intended to kill the mysterious gallery owner that impelled a bewildered Oisin to seek out the Luchettas as a matter of some importance. He had been putting off venturing to where they lived in the leafy suburb for various reasons. Even though he would not admit it to anyone, Mary's behaviour worried him. Her disappearances during the day and her uncontrolled outbursts when they did meet up further increased this concern for a sister he used to like. Their youth was long past. Mary had become something of a stranger to him. But she was his sister after all and deserved some loyalty.

It is the universal dilemma. How much can we be the keeper of another soul, no matter how dear they are to us? Mary had trod her own path and it had been a troubled one from all accounts. Now Oisin felt a terrible weight had suddenly been placed upon his shoulders with Mary's revelation. Her words chilled him. Her eyes had turned cold as she spoke those words. The power of the words and the manner in which they were said convinced him that she was serious in her intention. She meant to kill Anton Le Bon, the gallery owner. How and when she planned to carry this out was unknown. That she would do it was not.

It occurred to the troubled Oisin that the best course of action would be to keep a close watch on his sister while they were together. His return to Australia was imminent and he could not remain much longer in Edinburgh. Meeting the Luchettas might just distract Mary from her murderous mission. All these plans might go awry if the Luchettas no longer lived at 42 Willow Crescent. But it was worth a visit and he made up his mind to ask Mary to accompany him. They would catch the bus together and if he could remember the house, knock on the door and hope for the best.

Circumstances at the B and B prevented talking over breakfast as the owner, who previously had shown little attention in the brother and sister, began to fuss over them, and appeared to show an interest now in their daily plans. Neither Oisin nor Mary, however, had any wish to disclose any ideas they might have. Because her two guests had now stayed with her for a few weeks and decided to stay for a while longer, she decided that they were a safe bet as far as income was concerned. Things had been a bit lean for her financially over the autumn and winter months and she was eager to appear interested in what they were doing. Had she been aware of Mary's murderous announcement and Oisin's baffled response, she may have been less likely to extend the hand of friendship to the pair.

Mary ate a hearty breakfast much to the surprise of both Oisin and the B and B owner. Of late, she just picked at her food, and nine times out of ten stood up from the breakfast table and disappeared without a word to anyone. Oisin began to wonder if this was the right time to bring up the subject of the Luchettas. Mary's moods could change in a second but today she seemed relaxed, even jovial.

'Fancy a stroll to the Gardens?' he asked as they both stood up from table for the plates were already cleared away and the B and B owner was nowhere in sight. Much to his surprise, Mary agreed and locked her arm in his.

'What a good idea,' she replied. 'We haven't seen much of each other these past few days, have we now?'

Brother and sister strolled towards the Princes Street Gardens seemingly without a care in the world. A fine grey mist descended upon them in the late morning but did nothing to change the good humour that now existed between the two. Mary talked nonstop, a different woman than the day before, and Oisin relaxed just a little. Listening to her was the Mary of his childhood and memories of a happier time. The park was busy and most of the benches were occupied. They ambled along at a leisurely pace past the floral clock looking for somewhere to sit. Further along the path they spied a bench where a mother and a little lad of about two years of age were busy feeding the pigeons grains of seed from a brown paper bag. The boy took a handful of seeds and threw them onto the path. This brought five more pigeons to the scene. The birds flew off when two aggressive looking black headed gulls disturbed them. The commotion caused the mother to order the boy back onto the bench beside her. She and the boy then slid along the seat to make room for Oisin and Mary to sit down. The mother didn't speak; she just cast a rather resigned and weary smile in their direction. If this was Ballybeg, Oisin thought there would be an animated conversation about feeding birds and coping with toddlers. Not so, in the city. People were too busy here, rushing around, to bother with the infinite possibilities that these encounters could bring. Out of the blue, Kilgoolga came into his mind and how the raucous bird sounds in Australia were so different there. He suddenly missed the wide open space of his adopted country, and his wife, too. This business with Mary was delaying his return. Best to try to resolve the problem of Mary as soon as he could, then he could book his flight home to Kilgoolga and see Claire again. He might even tell her about the boy and the pigeons. People didn't feed the birds much out there, and when flocks of budgerigars landed on the wheat, the farmers shot them.

He judged this would be a good enough time to bring up the subject of the Luchetta family. He was about to speak but just at that moment the boy let out a shriek of delight, slid off the bench and moved at high speed towards a rather mangy looking grey squirrel. The squirrel, seeing the boy chasing him leapt first onto the arm of the bench where Mary was sitting and then with one almighty jump, scaled the tree behind them. The boy started to howl. The mother, now apologetic, gathered up her bags and took hold of the boy's hand with a very firm grip. The boy was having none of it. His was a full-on tantrum and he threw himself down onto the path, howling uncontrollably. The mother was now embarrassed as people passing by had to sidestep around the boy. A woman with grey hair, obviously a grandmother type, offered some advice to the distracted mother and, as if by magic, the boy stopped yelling and took his mother's hand. The two of them then proceeded to walk at a slow pace along the path towards the Walter Scott Memorial.

'Well, what do you make of that, Oisin?' Mary asked. 'Makes me glad I never had kids.'

'Would ye have liked to?'

'No.'

There was an awkward silence between them. No one else sat on their bench and Oisin took a deep breath.

'Mary', he said after a few more minutes. 'I want to tell ye something.'

'Oh, aye. Confession time, is it? Ye have a stack of fatherless kids scattered from here to the other side of the earth!'

'Nothing like that, Mary dear,' he grinned that lopsided grin that so endeared him to the women. 'No, I wanted to tell ye the reasons I came to Edinburgh forty years ago. You so wanted to come with me, to get away from Ballybeg, ye said. But I was on a mission then. Can ye remember much of Uncle Mick? Well, he was on his death bed and he entrusted me with an almighty secret. ' He was silent, remembering. A few seconds passed until he continued talking softly this time. It was as if he didn't want anyone around to hear. He was glad that the mother and the boy had wandered off and no one else had sat down beside them. 'This time, it's different, being here. This one is for myself,' he said.

'You always talked in riddles,' Mary pouted.

'And ye could always be relied upon to figure them out, couldn't ye?' Oisin replied with a good natured wink.

'I've always liked ye, Oisin,' she said.

He thought she was about to cry and he took hold of her hand. This was a different Mary from the one who just a few weeks ago had stabbed in the chest with her umbrella.

The fine mist had given way to fine rain. People hurried past anxious to get away from the shower.

Oisin stood up.

'C'mon, Mary,' he said. 'I'll shout ye to a coffee and cake. I've discovered a great little place off Princes Street an' I've been indulging meself there, so I have. Coffee to die for. Remember Mammy never would drink coffee, just tea? In that brown teapot an' the fancy one she brought out when we had visitors.'

'Aye. I remember. I don't drink tea now, just coffee.'

'Times change.'

'Aye, that they do. Funny how something said like that can make ye remember something else. Do you miss Mammy, Oisin?'

'Of course I do. She was one in a million was our mother. But her time had come.'

'What will it be like to die, Oisin?'

'Come now, Mary. Enough of that. Let's get out of the rain and have that coffee.'

He gave her hand a gentle squeeze. She wouldn't look at him but when she lifted her head, he noticed that one tiny tear had escaped and now positioned itself below her left eye. She seemed embarrassed by this display of emotion in front of her brother for she fumbled for a tissue in her handbag, blew her nose loudly and wiped the offending tear away. Mary was so unpredictable. It had to be a worry.

They walked from the park in silence towards the coffee lounge off Princes Street. *Coffee and Cake* had to be one of the most unpretentious establishments in Edinburgh for it was tucked away behind a line of shops with shrubbery in pots at the entrance making it almost hidden from view. It well and truly off the tourist track. Oisin had discovered it by accident. He thought it was one of Edinburgh's best kept secret. The coffee was out of this world and the array of mouth-watering cakes on display made choosing difficult. He had ventured back a few times and now he was pleased to bring Mary. He hoped the coffee combined with the atmosphere of the place would help her relax just a little, even be more rational. She was tense most of the time these days.

The coffee lounge was quiet when they entered. Tables were set out so that people and staff had room to move around them with ease. The room was brightly lit with sepia photographs in ornate frames of old Edinburgh on the walls. Oisin and Mary sat down at the table set for two below a photograph of horse drawn trams along Princes Street and Edinburgh Castle in the background. They had chosen a corner table at the front of the room. Here they could be observers as people came and went. It was an ideal place to talk.

Oisin's attention was drawn to four middle aged

women at the next table and he whispered to Mary that they all looked the same. 'Have to be Morningside ladies,' he said with a grin. Their styled hair and jewellery would have cost a small fortune. The women spoke with the well-modulated Scots accents of the moneyed class and Oisin, ever the observer was amused by their behaviour. Mary, however, wasn't the slightest bit interested. Her eyes were on the enormous piles of cakes on display.

'This place looks expensive, Oisin. Did you make your fortune out there in Australia? To afford a place like this?'

'Not so much my fortune but guess I did alright. Don't regret it. Was the right decision at the right time... but I didn't come here to talk about me. Anyhow, I just want to treat ye to the best coffee and cake I've ever tasted.' He smiled but Mary looked uncomfortable. Her attention was still focussed on the cakes. 'Ye choose a cake at the counter and order a coffee there as well. Then they bring your order over to ye at the table. All very modern. Let's see what's on offer today and then we can talk.'

Brother and sister approached the counter. Cakes were displayed on two rows, arranged with military precision and side by side on fancy plates, each and every one of them tempting the eager diner for wasn't this a wonderful display of self-indulgence? Who amongst us doesn't like cakes?

Chocolate cake, red velvet cake, coffee cake, fruit cake, black forest gateau, pineapple upside down cake and a tempting lemon drizzle cake, all competing to tempt the taste buds. Mary was a child again, overwhelmed and indecisive.

'You choose,' she said to Oisin.

Then she returned to sit at their table and waited patiently.

When Oisin returned to the table having made the decision for both of them, a large slice of chocolate cake and one equally huge portion of coffee cake, and ordered two expresso coffees, he thought Mary was close to tears for some reason he couldn't fathom. To avoid too much emotion in this refined establishment, he decided it was the right time to tell her about the Luchettas and his reason for returning to Edinburgh. So the tale was told while they waited for their order.

'I liked them all,' he said after he finished the story, 'especially Rosa and Concetta... Concetta, Uncle Mick's daughter. They were a very welcoming family, even Silvio wasn't so frightening when I got to know him a bit. I just want to find out what happened to them, that' all.'

'I knew nothing of any of this.'

'No. But now ye do. Would you like to come with me out to 42 Willow Crescent? I need to know. They could have moved on, who knows? Rosa and Silvio would have to be dead… it's forty years after all… but the young ones might be there. Silvio's daughter was Isabella, something of an enigma she was… but who knows? It's worth a bus ride, don't you think?'

Mary nodded her head just as the cakes and coffee arrived. Brother and sister ate in silence, both thinking their own thoughts. It was the closest the two of them had been in years. *The wonder of cake and coffee*, thought Oisin.

'I'd like to come with you, Oisin,' Mary said when they had finished eating. 'There's always been secrets hanging over our family, hasn't there?'

'Aye. Another time. Another place.'

'The past is the past, Oisin but it can come back to haunt us sometimes… can't it?'

'True words indeed. Maybe wanting to meet the Luchettas again is part of that. Part of my past. Maybe best forgotten?' He looked troubled.

Mary placed her hand on his arm. This was the Mary he remembered before time and circumstance got in the way. He smiled.

'Aye,' he said. 'Why not? Let's recapture the past for once. Who knows what we'll discover. The house mightn't even be there and no one remembers anything of the Luchettas. But then I'll know once and for all.'

They got up ready to leave. It was lunchtime and the coffee lounge had filled up now and there was a queue at the door waiting to enter. People apparently could eat cake at any time. It was then that Mary changed.

A short, stocky man in his sixties accompanied by a tall, elegant woman who looked to be an Italian had entered the room. Instead of waiting in the queue the man pushed his way through the line of people to a table set in a private part of the room. The woman moved as elegant as a prima ballerina, her head held high, her arm tucked into her companion's. She was no stranger to making an appearance in a public place for she was seemingly unaware of the effect that the two of them had on the waiting crowd. People moved aside to let them pass. When they reached the table they were immediately attended to by a man of about forty years of age. This man graciously held the chair for the woman to sit down. He bowed to both the man and the woman. The short stocky man and the woman sat down.

Still Mary did not move. When Oisin tried to take her arm, she made no sound nor did she acknowledge him. Instead, she stared in the direction of the man and woman who by now had settled themselves comfortably at the private table and were deep in conversation. It was though Mary Kelly had seen a ghost. Without another word, she left the table, leaving a slightly bewildered Oisin to pay for their coffee and cake.

CHAPTER TWELVE

Isabella Luchetta moved slower these days. Her youth was long gone and it had to be said that the years had not been kind to Isabella. Frail, white-haired and approaching ninety years of age, she relied on a walking stick for support and cursed when she couldn't climb the stairs. She thought old age a tiresome inconvenience and grumbled at the young.

Isabella had never been considered a beauty. As a young woman her thick black hair was styled in such a severe style that she was often mistaken for a man. What with masculine looking facial features and short statue this misunderstanding could be forgiven but to Isabella it further enhanced her disdain for physical beauty. In fact, it made her even more determined to dress in a way not considered acceptable within her social class. This rebellion, for that was what it was, caused many an argument between herself and her aristocratic father, Silvio who was always immaculately turned out even when lounging in his own home. Comparisons were made between herself and her cousin, Concetta who had none of Isabella's rebellious nature, and was considered by all and sundry to be an Italian beauty. Comparisons were often drawn between Concetta and the actress, Sophia Loren. To make matters even worse for Isabella, people liked Concetta and they were wary around the unpredictable Isabella. This caused all manner of arguments in the Luchetta household. It normally ended with Isabella storming off, threatening never to set foot in the house again.

Isabella was Silvio's only child and therefore destined to inherit the olive groves and vineyards in their native Italy. Although Isabella and her father both knew that Silvio would have preferred a son to take over the business affairs, it was just one of those things to be accepted, if somewhat grudgingly on Silvio's part. However, Isabella's lack of beauty was somehow a compensation for this if all had gone according to plan. She was, after all, rather a masculine looking woman. Alas, Silvio's plan failed dismally. Headstrong and stubborn Isabella had little interest in the olive groves and vineyards preferring life in Edinburgh and the company of the unemployed bartender, Patrick Allsop.

Isabella was aware of Patrick's feelings towards her but it made no difference to her. She accepted the fact that he stayed with her for her money and she turned a blind eye to his many affairs with other women. After these dalliances, as Patrick called them, he would beg Isabella to forgive him and assure her it would never happen again. Then, on bended knee he would propose marriage to her. She always refused. Marriage to Isabella was a trap for women and of little advantage to them if the truth be told. It was the men who benefitted most from this arrangement in Isabella's opinion. No way would she agree to a legal binding with Patrick. She loved him but didn't trust him and she held a tight rein on the money strings. This fact alone would have been some comfort to her father who lived in hope that it was not too late for his wilful daughter to see the error of her ways, take over the family business and leave the gigolo Patrick for good, for this is what Silvio and the rest of the family called her lover behind his back.

This weakness of character in Patrick further angered her father, Silvio but no manner of persuasion could bring Isabella to separate from her feckless lover. When Silvio threatened to disinherit Isabella and leave the olive groves and the vineyards in Bologna to Concetta and her children, Isabella flew into a rage and father and daughter didn't speak to each other for six years only to be reunited, somewhat unemotionally at the funeral of Concetta's mother, Rosa Cavellessi.

Isabella and Patrick endured a stormy twenty years or so together until Patrick was run over by an out of control and drunken driver one dark winter evening. He stumbled as he tried to cross the Grassmarket not aware of the oncoming vehicle.

The famous Grassmarket, where so many executions, murders and riots had taken place was once again the scene of a tragedy. The drunken driver, apparently too inebriated to notice the pedestrian in front of him, caught sight of him at that brief fatal moment and tried to halt the vehicle by braking hard, but the unfortunate Patrick who himself was a little the worse for wear, was thrown onto the bonnet of the vehicle due to the sudden braking and he landed face down on the cobbles. The driver reversed in a panic, then accelerated forwards, consequently driving over and crushing Patrick's right arm and shoulder as he did so. Apparently now fully aware of what he had done, the driver escaped from the scene at high speed. Two men who had witnessed the incident rushed to try to help Patrick, one dialled the emergency services and in record time Patrick was at the Edinburgh Infirmary but unfortunately it was too late. He died from his injuries a few hours later with a distraught Isabella by his side. The drunken driver escaped justice for he was never located despite major police involvement.

After a tragedy there is often a blessing, even a rebirth. Although no one in the Luchetta family had liked Patrick the effect of his death on Isabella brought the family together for a short time. She and her father talked to each other as they once had done before Patrick came on the scene. This time the subject of the olive groves and the vineyards were once again on the agenda. Isabella agreed that she should travel to Italy to discuss matters with Concetta and her Spanish husband, Ramon. They had taken over the running of business enterprise after Isabella had shown no interest. A reconciliation of some sorts was the result of the meeting between the two women. Unfettered from the restraints that Patrick had imposed upon her for over twenty years, the indomitable Isabella discovered that she did have her father's way with business. Much to everyone's amazement she began to take an active interest in the olive groves and the vineyards, even developing a liking for the grapes in particular. Her ideas for the wine that came from the vines were inspirational. It was as if a light bulb had been turned on in Isabella's brain. She spent more time in Italy. The result was that the business which had been just ticking along in a steady way expanded thanks to Isabella. She enlisted the aid of a cousin of Silvio to help manage the workers as more people were needed to be employed especially in the summer months. Like her father, Isabella believed in the power of family members, not outsiders, to control business dealings. Almost overnight the Luchetta family, who were always considered rich, suddenly became very rich.

It appeared that all was going well for Isabella. And so it did for a few years.

As she aged, her lack of beauty took on a new side for her. She held her head high and directed her employees with a determination that had been her father's mantra. In this, she gained respect from both her family and her workers. Ever optimistic Concetta who seemed to have inherited some of her Irish father's genes for it has to be noted that Mick Kelly when he had a few Guinness in him did indeed have a sense of humour, appeared relieved not to have the total responsibility that owning the vineyards and the olive groves required.

All was going well for the wealthy Luchettas. Until one day tragedy struck a few years later when Silvio suffered a major heart attack and never regained consciousness. His death was so unexpected that it shook the family and everyone else. He was no longer there and he left a gap that could never be filled. All of a sudden, Isabella was now the matriarch with neither her lover nor her father any longer by her side. When she turned seventy-five years of age she decided to hand her share of the business over to Concetta's son and retire in style back to her beloved Edinburgh.

****

As Oisin and Mary wandered along the leafy suburb where Willow Crescent was located, past the palatial mansions set back from the road behind hedges and stone walls, Oisin began to doubt the wisdom of returning to the place that had held such happy memories for him forty years ago. Nostalgia can play tricks on the mind and seduce us into thinking that the past which we can never return to, was indeed a happier time. A stranger in Edinburgh all those years ago, Oisin had found solace with the wealthy Luchetta family. He had been a frequent visitor and a very welcome one at that. But that was then.

It was a tantalising thought that got hold of him when he made the hasty decision to return to the Scottish capital after his mother's death in Ballybeg. In Edinburgh he hoped to try to recapture some of the comfort he had felt with the Luchetta family then. Of course, forty years is a long time and he was certain that the older members of the family whose companionship and hospitality he had enjoyed so much would be no longer living but it was a secret hope that the younger ones he knew then might be around, and welcome him with the enthusiasm that they had done in the past. But as he approached 42 Willow Crescent and viewed the black ornate wrought iron gates he remembered with such clarity, nervousness took hold of him, and he hesitated. He remembered how he tried to open the large gates the first time he had visited. Puzzled, he then noticed there was a smaller pedestrian gate crafted in the same wrought iron design further along the wall. The small gate opened easily and this was the entrance he had used from then on. The small gate was still there looking none the worse for wear and no longer in use. He decided to try the larger gate.

Mary was no help in any of this. She had been surly all morning and hardly spoke to him. She viewed his mission into reminiscence nothing but a foolish whim. She had agreed to accompany him on one condition that he got it over with as quickly as possible. So much had happened in those forty years in her own life and the story of her Uncle Mick and his hidden love affair with the Italian woman, Rosa, the result of which was the arrival of Concetta, their daughter, was of little consequence to her. She hardly remembered her difficult Uncle Mick. Oisin's need to meet with the Luchetta family and this being his sole reason to return to Edinburgh before returning to Australia was to her troubled mind an obsession of sorts. She thought it was unlikely that the Italian family still lived in the address where they now stood and Oisin, as usual was chasing after windmills like Don Quixote.

'Is this the place, Oisin?' she asked. She noticed

that he looked a little unsure and a frown had appeared on his brow.

'I think so,' was the reply. 'The gates are the same although the trees have grown up behind the wall.'

'Well? Do you want to go in or are we going to stand outside like two idiots?'

'I'm not sure now.'

'Oisin. You can be so annoying some time. You said this was the sole reason you wanted to come to Edinburgh. Now, you don't know what to do. At least, I know why *I* wanted to come here,' she concluded and her face took on a dark expression.

Her words were enough for Oisin to make a decision. He took hold of the latch on the large gate and pushed it open ahead of Mary. It was the same gravel drive he remembered with well-tended gardens and acacias of various varieties, yew trees and the boxwood, all grown higher now, and the evergreens with their dense foliage which made such crisp topiary shapes. The large cedar trees that had obscured the house from the street had grown larger. One had been cut down and now just a stump remained, a solitary reminder of how transient is life. It was like walking into a dream.

The three worn stone steps were there; the stone Doric pillars standing like silent sentinels beside them, and the impressive solid oak door, all were the same as his memory of them. The boar's head brass door handle was still there in the centre of the door. He remembered how he had wondered which bell he should use, and then he had decided to ring the other bell set in the stone. This bell was one of those old fashioned ones common to the larger houses; the brass button to press the bell set inside a black cast iron circular frame. Oisin remembered how everything brass in the house was kept polished to perfection, including the door handle and this button which rang the bell. He hesitated.

'Oh, hurry up, Oisin and ring the wretched bell.'

This was the Mary of his youth speaking, petulant, bossy and annoying all at the same time. He pressed the button.

A few minutes later the door opened just enough to reveal an elderly, rather rounded woman with untidy grey hair and a face that looked as if it had seen many a woe. The woman held the door with one hand. The other hand was on her Zimmer frame.

'What do you want?' She asked in a rather offhand manner as if she was tired of opening the door to strangers.

'Do any of the Luchetta family still live here?'

'Who's asking?'

'Oisin Kelly from Ireland and this is my sister,

Mary. I knew the family years ago. In fact, I think we are distant cousins of Concetta....'

'I'll see if Isabella will see you. She's havin' a nap an' doesn't like to be disturbed. What did you say your name was?'

'Oisin Kelly.'

And the door was shut again.

So one member of the Luchetta family still lived here but what a change? Not one of the staff would have dared address any of the family in such a familiar way when Oisin knew them. It was definitely Signorina Isabella or Miss Isabella then.

Oisin was now feeling apprehensive and doubting the wisdom of this return into nostalgia. Maybe it is best to leave the past where it is. It is a foolish person who thinks by returning to old haunts, things will be the same. Life moves on. Just as he was about to whisper these thoughts to Mary, the door opened again.

'Isabella will see you. Follow me.'

She turned to Oisin and said, 'She's deaf, mind. You'll have to speak up.'

'Should make for an interesting conversation then,' replied Oisin with a grin. 'I'm deaf in one ear.'

The attempt at a joke made no difference to the woman with the Zimmer frame. She shuffled ahead of him with Mary following a few reluctant paces behind them both.

It was the same grand hallway of Oisin's memory with the plaster ceiling above and the dark oak panels below. They walked on the ornate floor tiles, not daring to utter a word. At the far end of the hall the bust of Giuseppe Garibaldi, the hero of Italy, sat there on the Carrara marble stand in the same position that he had always been. Above Garibaldi the splendid Luchetta Coat Of Arms, the fabric now showing signs of deterioration but the design still visible hung from the wall. On either side of the statue looking as if they had never moved in forty years were the two uncomfortable hall chairs. It was like walking into a time warp.

The room the dour woman with the Zimmer frame ushered them into was the same for Oisin too. Books filled the room as before. Most of them unread, gathering dust on shelves behind the glass doors. Oisin remembered he had never been encouraged to touch any of them but then, he had more things to think about, the family secrets from Mick and sex with Cecy had occupied most of his thoughts. He never brought the American girl to meet the Luchettas, she was his secret then, and still was, and would be until his dying day.

Isabella Luchetta, frail and tiny in the large armchair, opened her eyes when she was awakened by the hand that held the Zimmer frame.

'People to see you, Isabella. Do you want tea?'

The dark brown eyes of her father stared at the two strangers. The eyes, still bright, the head held just as high, her white hair cropped as before, this was the formidable Isabella of memory. Oisin bowed his head slightly and held out his hand.

'Miss Luchetta,' he said. 'I don't know whether ye will remember me? I was a frequent visitor here... forty years ago... I knew your father, Silvio and your Aunt Rosa... Concetta and the children, too. We became friends and the hospitality of your family is something I have never forgotten. I was young then and your family made me welcome.'

'Sit.' Isabella waved her hand in the direction of the two chairs positioned at either side of her, and then she said, 'Bring us some tea and those iced cakes, Aggie.'

The woman and the Zimmer frame shuffled past.

'She is the cook,' said Isabella. She sniffed and blew her nose with a white linen handkerchief.

Oisin and Mary sat on the faded fabric armchairs as directed. The only sound in the room came from the mantelpiece clock, a rather ornate looking object with a second hand and gold numerals. Oisin glanced at the clock. It was ten minutes to eleven. They had taken over an hour to reach 42 Willow Crescent from their Bread and Breakfast.

'What did you say your name was?' The penetrating brown eyes fixed on Oisin's face and despite the forty years since he had last seen them, he felt slightly intimidated as he had been then.

'Oisin Kelly from Ireland.'

'Speak up. I am a little hard of hearing these days.'

Oisin repeated his words and this time he turned his head so he could hear Isabella better with his good ear.

'Ah. Ireland. My father was a frequent visitor there. I never had any desire to visit the place.' Turning to Mary she asked, 'And who is this?'

'Apologies, Miss Luchetta. I'm forgetting my manners. This is my sister, Mary.'

'Ah. Brother and sister. There is a family resemblance. My cousin, Concetta has the same nose.'

'Concetta's father was my Uncle Mick,' Oisin said.

'I remember you now. It enraged my father that his sister could have been so foolish as to take a lover, she being a married woman, but then my father was set in his patriarchal ways. I admired my Aunt Rosa for her courage. We women can be as wild as wolves sometimes, do you not agree, Mary Kelly?'

Mary, who up to that moment had taken little

interest in the conversation, nodded her head but said nothing.

Oisin who was by now beginning to feel a little out of place amongst this sign of female solidarity decided to change the subject.

'I live in Australia now,' he said. 'In the outback town of Kilgoolga. Been there forty years.'

'Our mother has just died,' Mary interrupted. 'My brother was her favourite. Oisin deigned to return for her funeral.'

'Don't be like that, Mary. I would have come home anyway and... I'm not sure I was Mother's favourite.'

'Of course you were. She was the one she held on for before she popped off. None of us mattered but you. Oisin this, Oisin that.'

Isabella heard most of the sibling rivalry. It amused her. The brother and sister bickering reminded her of her and Concetta. They were cousins but they had grown up together, lived in the same house as children, and were jealous of each other most of the time.

'Was there any reason that you wanted to see me?' Isabella asked. 'Forty years is a long time to renew acquaintances.'

'I accept that, Miss Luchetta... '

Isabella interrupted. 'You may call me Isabella. We appear to have a slight family connection. Times have changed, Mr Kelly. Everyone calls me Isabella these days... even the cook.'

Oisin grinned. 'Well then,' he said, 'Isabella, ye may call me Oisin.'

Eighty-five year old Isabella laughed.

'Touché,' she said.

That was the moment that Oisin relaxed. He sank back into the armchair and all the feelings of siting in this room came back to him.

'To answer your question, I came to see if any of the Luchetta family still lived here. So glad you are. You see, Isabella I was happy in this house... happier here than I had ever been anywhere. Coming here after all those years I probably wanted to recapture some of that happiness. It's an existential thing I think... and I became very fond of your Aunt Rosa. She treated me like a son.'

'She was a good woman.'

'Aye. That she was.'

All this time Mary had sat without moving or speaking. Her eyes were fixed on the wall and she only moved when the cook with the Zimmer frame entered the room. It appeared that the cook had become somewhat adept at balancing a tray and pushing her Zimmer frame at the same time. This tray with teapot, milk jug, sugar bowl and three cups and saucers was held with her left hand whilst her right hand manoeuvred the frame. Watching the precarious operation, Oisin had a devilish thought, *Only the Luchettas would employ a cook with a Zimmer frame?* He stood up and asked to help but his offer was ignored. Instead the cook spoke to Isabella.

'I'm bringin' in them cakes you like now,' she said, and shuffled off to return a few minutes later holding another tray with two plates on it. A dainty selection of iced cakes was on one tray and piled high on the other one a mouth-watering selection of Italian biscuits. The cakes and the hospitality in this house was just the same as it had been forty years ago for Oisin. He was glad now that he had made the effort to visit. Memories of the tasty almond crescent shaped biscuits with their sugar coating came back to him, and how Rosa had insisted he take more for she said he was a growing boy and needed to keep his strength up. He had obliged her with his Irish banter as he did so. To his delight, the same biscuits were on the tray alongside some rectangular shaped ones.

Isabella poured the tea and offered the cakes. Mary did not move. She sipped her tea in the fine china cup and shook her head when the cakes and biscuits were offered. Oisin had no such reticence. He devoured two iced cakes and three sugary biscuits. When tea was offered again, his cup was filled to the top. No one spoke whilst all this was going on. It gave Oisin time to look around the room.

There is something about returning to a place after a long absence that enters into your soul. This surely was the case for Oisin. The room in which he sat was much the same as his recollection of it. The same paintings hung on the wall, oils and watercolours of bucolic rural scenes, and here and there a few ancestor's faces peered out behind heavy wooden frames; the plaster ceiling high above his head with its ornate embossed floral design set in the centre with the border line of flowers, the design so elegant, so reminiscent of decorative Italian ceilings in the larger houses; even the thick beige curtains, open now to reveal casement windows and the view into the garden, all this was there, and something more that caught his eye. On the wall behind where Mary was seated there was another painting, and this one was so out of place in this faded room where the past was captured, and locked there in that time of Oisin's memory.

For behind a silver metal frame and under glass was a very modern work of art. Mounted on the wall beside all the ancestral paintings, this one was larger, more dramatic, its presence announcing, and somewhat with hope, that the past had been banished in this room. Here was the future. The grey winged horse bounding through rings of red and gold had galloped into the room.

'That painting, Isabella... the one on the wall behind Mary? Was that done by Francesca Fitzwilliam?' He spoke louder so that the elderly Italian woman could hear him.

Isabella laughed. 'I believe so... an up and coming young artist so they say. Do you know of her?'

'Aye that I do. I bought one of her paintings just the other day. A smaller one.'

He thought that he couldn't have afforded the larger paintings but then Isabella was a rich woman.

'A daughter of a good friend of mine from Bologna decided that the room needed something modern in it. Sophia always has an eye for a work of art. I said to her, "These paintings of a winged horse. I read once that a horse moving like that spelt Death. Are you giving me a hint?" Sophia laughed and replied that this artist will go far for Francesca has imagination combined with artistic excellence. She got a bargain, she said, but then she bought the painting from *Le Bon,* and no doubt did *indeed* get a bargain... perhaps a huge discount... or it might have been a gift.'

Isabella sniffed and lifted her head slightly.

'I do not gossip but the painting came to me in rather a suspicious manner. It was given to me, you see. I wondered at the generosity at the time. Sophia has been in a somewhat irregular relationship for many years, although she is married to a count, but then everyone is aware of Count di Laguna's preferences. Sophia's mother, my dear friend sadly passed away last year, and I must say she was somewhat distressed with her daughter's situation. We often discussed it over a coffee in Bologna. But then Sophia can be quite wilful at times and would not take advice from anyone.'

Oisin decided it was better not to pursue this somewhat intriguing story. He had never heard of a Sophia di Laguna nor did he know the famous Anton Le Bon although he guessed he had briefly seen the man in the gallery.

'I plan to give my winged horse to my daughter, Suze when I return to Australia next week. She is something of an artist,' he concluded rather lamely. Suze's talent was questionable to be truthful but she did appreciate the finer things in life.

'Ah, yes. That is interesting. I think Sophia may have done the right thing for me this time. I find looking at the winged horse with all its colour and abstract design strangely reassuring. The bright colours of this painting make a welcome change from the oils of the ancestors and the watercolours of Scotland and Italy, don't you think? Certainly this artist has talent... but then that art dealer always had an eye for gifted artists... and I have to say, of particular interest if they were attractive young women.'

All this time Mary had not said a word. She sat without moving a muscle, holding the full cup of tea and saucer on her lap - not drinking it, just staring. Her silence rather unnerved the usually talkative Oisin but any time he tried to bring his sister into the conversation, his attempts failed. What was going on inside her head? It was obvious that Mary had no interest in Isabella Luchetta, the conversation or being where she was. Oisin had thought that bringing her might have helped. He had talked to her in glowing terms about the Luchetta family, and Silvio and Rosa in particular, the kindness he had felt with them, and their hospitality when he was a young lad in Edinburgh. Instead, now she embarrassed him, and he was annoyed with her.

Isabella sighed. Her mind was back in another time and she wanted to tell someone about it. This astute Oisin Kelly might just be the one to hear. His odd sister had no interest in the conversation and probably wouldn't be bothered to listen anyway. Isabella had already forgotten the woman's name but she remembered Oisin. That was a name to remember.

'Oisin,' she whispered in a confidential way and moved her body towards him so he could hear what she had to say. 'There was a man once... his name was Anton Le Bon...'

Everything changed at that precise moment. Mary moved. She screamed, clenched a fist and yelled, 'BASTARD'... and... 'YOU BLOODY BASTARD' ... then without looking at either Isabella or Oisin, threw her full cup of tea over the painting by Francesca Fitzwilliam.

The fine porcelain cup with the floral design broke into dozens of small pieces; the tea gushed like a flood over the glass which secured the painting behind it; the liquid dripped down the wall destroying the faded wallpaper of a thousand summers. Then Mary fled, almost colliding with the cook and her Zimmer frame, who at that moment was entering the room, unaware of the commotion. Everyone heard Mary's footsteps in the hall, and then the front door slamming.

Mortified, embarrassed beyond belief and at a loss for words, Oisin tried in a clumsy fashion to retrieve pieces of the shattered cup whilst all the time Isabella remained seating, her face showing no emotion whatsoever. Finally she spoke,

'Leave it,' she said. 'Perhaps you had better rescue your sister... don't you think?'

CHAPTER THIRTEEN

Isabella did not move after Oisin left. Instead she remained seated in her chair while the cook fussed over the broken cup, the tea now drying on the painting and the wallpaper below.

'What was all that about?' grumbled the sullen cook. 'The wallpaper's ruined. It's a wonder the glass didn't smash on this here painting? Bloody cheek if you ask me.'

She started to pick up pieces of the porcelain. This was quite an acrobatic feat considering that she had to hold the frame with one hand and bend almost double to locate the broken fragments.

Isabella didn't answer. In fact, she hardly heard what the cook had to say. She had turned off her hearing aids and shut her eyes. She had things to remember. Anton Le Bon came into her mind first. She saw his young face in her mind's eye as if he was in the room with her. The years since then had gone by, and lately with increasing speed as she aged, she concluded but then at her age, that had to be expected. The days she spent at her father's vineyards with the olive trees growing on the hillside sometimes seemed another life away from now. But there was her friendship with Beatrice Caputo to remember, a friendship that began when the two girls were both eighteen years of age, and lasted until Beatrice's death.

Beatrice married a man she loved. Isabella wasn't so fortunate with Patrick. Beatrice had a daughter, Sophia, her only child, whilst Isabella was childless much to her father's displeasure. Both women were fighters in their own way and cared deeply for each other. It was an enduring and altogether admirable thing and much envied, for although Isabella and Beatrice had long periods apart, they always connected like peas in a pod when they met up again.

After Patrick's death Isabella travelled to Bologna more frequently, often remaining at the Luchetta home for six months or so while she learned more about the family business. It was then that a routine was established between herself and Beatrice that was satisfying to them both for they would meet once a fortnight for a coffee either at the Caputo apartment in Bologna or at one of the many cafés that were dotted around the town. It was there at one of these delightful establishments that Isabella first set eyes on Anton Le Bon.

Isabella and Beatrice, now both well into their forties, and half a lifetime of experiences to ponder over, had seated themselves at a table facing the Piazza Maggiore where they could enjoy the bustling atmosphere and the constant flow of human traffic. The women spoke in English with a smattering of Italian phrases thrown in every now and then. Beatrice was recounting a particularly amusing episode in her life with her husband when they both had had a little too much of the vino, and, as she was about to finish the story which had taken a long time to tell as the two women were laughing so much, she stopped speaking, and spoke in a rather acerbic voice,

'Why, there's Sophia and she's with *that* boy.'

Sophia arrived at their table hand in hand with a short and stocky boy with a black beard and shoulder length hair tied up in a ponytail. He didn't look at all like the sort of companion that the extroverted young girl would favour. Sophia kissed her mother first and then planted an equally familiar kiss on Isabella's cheek. She and the young man sat down.

'Isabella, this is my friend Anton Le Bon,' she spoke in Italian.

There are occasions in life when a person is introduced to us and we take an instant dislike to them. This happened the moment Isabella Luchetta met Anton Le Bon. She shook his hand and then nodded her head as was her way. Anton tightened his grip on Isabella's hand for just a second or two longer than was deemed polite. This one act resulted in Isabella, from that moment on, being wary in the company of Anton Le Bon. It was a gesture of control over women and Isabella remembered Patrick and the arguments they had had. Sophia, unaware of the subtle occurrence that had just occurred between her mother's friend and her lover, chatted on in her usual enthusiastic way before announcing that Anton was an artist and he had met Uncle Giovanni who had told him to become an art dealer instead.

Anton leaned back in his chair and twirled his fingers through Sophia's long black hair. To Isabella it seemed like a gesture that implied possession. Every now and then he would shift position so that he was closer to Sophia. Her response was to kiss him firmly on the lips. Her mother was uncomfortable at this public display of affection and her face revealed disapproval. It made no difference to the two lovers. In fact, it looked like Sophia was relishing annoying her mother for one of the kisses lasted for a minute or so until Anton broke away and, now stroking Sophia's neck, he said in that superior tone that he used when he was in the company of those he considered lesser mortals,

'Giovanni helped me to get established. He was right. I enjoy being an art dealer not an artist.'

This was news to Beatrice. She had no idea that her brother knew Anton but then the brother and sister rarely met although they both lived in Bologna. She was about to say something to that effect when Anton continued,

'I own a gallery in Brighton in the south of England and Giovanni suggested we open one here in Bologna. I'll see more of Sophia then.'

He kissed the back of Sophia's neck and she giggled.

'I plan to open my galleries worldwide. I've my eye on space in London next. The name of Le Bon will be a household name in the art world. Watch this space, ladies.'

He got up to leave and Sophia stood up with a shrug of the shoulders. She was relishing the disapproval her behaviour caused her mother, and probably Isabella as well. The two young people kissed once again, and then they wandered off hand in hand without a backward glance.

'It is time Sophia was married, Isabella. That boy is a bad influence on her I think. We have someone else in mind. Alexandro di Laguna has shown an interest and both our families approve.'

Isabella could only agree. Anton Le Bon was a bit too much like Patrick for her liking.

Sophia agreed to marry Alexandro di Laguna a few months after this conversation. It had to be one of the grandest of weddings ever held at the beautiful Bologna Cathedral. Bologna high society buzzed. The sun shone and the bride was a fairy tale princess on the arm of her new husband. Her mother shed a tear. Her father looked relieved... and Anton Le Bon was nowhere to be seen.

A few years later, Isabella met Anton Le Bon in an unexpected way. He was then in his thirties and true to his word; he had established himself as a gallery owner with a reputation for attracting new talent. He had opened a small gallery in upmarket Kensington and was promoting the work of a new artist, a young woman. Details of the opening night where her paintings would be exhibited were sent to Isabella at her Edinburgh address. Out of curiosity, she decided to accept.

The gallery was located in a side street and space certainly was limited. It appeared that Anton had gone for an address. No doubt as his reputation grew so would the size of his galleries. The room was crowded. Isabella recognised a few faces from the television and one or two other well-known figures. She accepted the glass of red wine offered to her by a young woman dressed in a white blouse and tight black skirt, and she looked around. Anton was nowhere to be seen. Isabella was no stranger to such gatherings, and she soon started a conversation with an elderly couple, who were keen to enlighten her about the talented new artist that the amazing Anton Le Bon had discovered. They were enthusiastic about the exhibition and there were a good many red stickers appearing besides her paintings. Isabella managed to break away from the couple to study a painting that had caught her eye. It was an interesting work. The artist had captured the greys and blues of a windswept sea scene in a unique way and Isabella considered whether to buy it or not. It was at the moment of indecision that she felt a hand upon her arm, and when she turned around, she saw that the hand belonged to none other than Anton Le Bon.

'Ah,' he said. 'That's an inspired piece of work, don't you agree?'

He was older but she recognised him at once. He had filled out and was now rather portly around the waist. The black beard and shoulder length hair along with the ponytail that he had in Bologna were gone. Now clean shaven and his hair trimmed to perfection but the dark brown eyes were the same. Seeing him at such close proximity, Isabella felt the same towards him as before.

'I've been admiring this work. Is the artist here?' She said.

'Yes indeed. Would you like to meet her?' He frowned slightly. 'I believe I have seen you before,' he said, 'in Bologna. I think we met one day at the Piazza Maggiore and you were with Signora Caputo. Ah, I remember now... am I right... Isabella Luchetta?'

He shook her hand, and Isabella felt the same

grip as before, that controlling gesture she disliked in a man.

'I remember you too,' replied Isabella and lifted her head. 'Anton Le Bon. And you *have* your gallery.'

'I have indeed and more to come,' he answered.

He took her arm in a familiar way much to Isabella's slight annoyance. 'Now we have to locate my young prodigy... '

The noise level in the gallery was getting worse and it took Anton a few minutes to locate his prodigy. The artist had positioned herself beside the wall at the back of the room, and she looked petrified.

Isabella, a keen observer of human nature, sensed that this young woman had never been exposed to anything like this before. The loud voices and the arrogance of some of the guests would be daunting for her. When Anton saw her, looking nervous and out of her depth, he showed no sympathy. Instead he said, 'Come now, Mary. You have to mingle... talk to people. I can't sell your paintings if you hide away like a frightened little mouse. People want to speak to the artist... that's half the reason they come to opening nights... as well as discovering new talent.'

As he spoke, he took hold of Mary's right arm and pushed her towards Isabella.

'I have someone you should meet now. Be a good girl and smile.'

Hearing his words, Isabella felt slightly uneasy. Here was a man who had control over this young girl.

'Mary, this lady likes your sea scape. Perhaps you can tell her where you got your inspiration from?'

Mary's face reddened. She bit her lip and then she mumbled, 'From Ireland.'

Isabella smiled.

'You have talent, my dear. My father was a frequent visitor to the west of Ireland. He always talked about the wild Atlantic seas. I can see where you would have got your inspiration from... although I've never been to Ireland myself.'

Hearing a sympathetic voice amongst all the noise, Mary relaxed just a little and smiled.

'I loved riding my pony along the sand, and sometimes my brother and I would just sit and watch the waves rolling in... although it's fierce weather in the winter, wild winds and the cold... sure there's none like it.'

'Mary, this is Signora Luchetta and I think she would like to view your painting.'

Taking hold of Mary's arm again, he pushed his way through the throng of noisy guests, speaking every now and then to those he recognised, until the three of them arrived at the painting under discussion.

Isabella had decided by then to buy the painting as a gift to her father. When they finally got to view the painting, there was a surprise.

'Well, well, what do you know, Mary Kelly,' Anton said and he did an unexpected thing. He whispered something into Mary's ear, and she blushed.

'I am sorry, Signora Luchetta, but it appears that this painting has just been sold.'

There was a round red sticker placed prominently beside the description. Anton looked pleased. He turned to Isabella, and then said in the imperious way that had become a characteristic of his since his fortune and reputation had grown, 'Maybe, we could interest you in something else...? Or a commission perhaps? I'm sure Mary Kelly would be happy to paint another seascape, wouldn't you, Mary darling?'

****

It took a few moments for Oisin to know what to do after Mary's unexpected outburst. He had felt the full force of her anger since his return to Ballybeg, and in Edinburgh as well, but he had never before seen her turn this fury in front of a stranger.

Muttering an apology to Isabella once again, he made a hasty exit to the front door, into the garden, and in his haste he almost forgot to close the heavy iron gate behind him. Out of breath now, he stood outside 42 Willow Crescent and looked up and down the street, hoping Mary might have waited at the bus stop a few hundred metres away. She was nowhere to be seen. He had no idea why she had turned her anger onto an innocent painting and in such a way as to cause embarrassment and bewilderment to everyone in so doing. Why did the name Anton Le Bon bring out a kind of madness within her for surely that was the reason for the outburst? It was after Isabella mentioned the name of the gallery owner that Mary reacted the way she did. He doubted if the name of the young artist, Francesca Fitzwilliam would have caused such a flare-up. When he showed her his own purchase of Francesca's painting, she had been quite appreciative and even congratulated him on his taste. This was something. Mary rarely praised anyone. No, it had to Anton Le Bon. And there was that other worry in Oisin's head. Mary had said that she intended to kill Anton Le Bon.

He walked faster now towards the bus stop but there was no sign of a bus so he decided to would walk the five miles or so into town thinking that this might have been the route that Mary might have taken. It was an almighty guess though. In Mary's state she could be anywhere.

A man of about fifty years of age walking a large black and brown Rottweiler dog on a lead greeted him with a nod. Oisin decided to enquire about Mary.

'Excuse me,' he said in his polite way, 'I wonder if ye have seen a woman in a hurry running along the street?'

'Can't say I have, mate,' the man answered with a grin. 'Have you lost your missus?'

'No. No. She's my sister.'

'Och well, she'll turn up. How old is she?'

'About sixty.'

'Think she's old enough now to look after herself, don't you?'

Oisin, in normal times would have enjoyed the banter, but he was becoming more distressed thinking about the behaviour of Mary, so he just thanked the man and left him before any more conversation could take place between them.

Walking faster now, Oisin arrived at the main thoroughfare into the town. Although he was in a constant state of looking to the left and the right in the feeble hope that he might suddenly come across his unpredictable sister, he doubted that he would find her along the busy street. There were too many people about jostling for space along the pavement.

Mary could have gone into a coffee lounge or a shop, or anywhere for that matter. He decided that his best bet was to head back to the Bed and Breakfast. It was getting later in the day and she would surely have to make her way back there at some point. Poor Oisin was quite worried.

But Mary was not at the B and B. Tired from his hasty walk, he flopped onto the bed and much to his surprise, fell asleep to be awakened an hour or so later by a knock on the door. It was the B and B owner, and she wanted to know if he and his sister would be requiring an evening meal? Oisin, half asleep, shook his head. Then he asked whether she had seen Mary?

'No, Oisin,' was the reply. 'An Austrian couple just booked in for a week, and they'll be wantin' an evening meal tonight, so I thought I'd ask if you'd like one too. I heard ye comin' up to your room, ken...but naw, I haven't seen hide nor hair of your sister. Expect she's out shoppin'...'

Oisin and Mary had been with her a month now and she was fond of Oisin. He was a likeable sort of fellow. She wasn't so friendly towards Mary though but she didn't like to say too much. To keep guests coming, it paid to be courteous.

'I expect ye are right sure enough. She'll turn up when she's good an' ready,' Oisin replied but he wasn't convinced.

That evening he walked the streets of Edinburgh. There was still no sight of Mary and he began to despair. Any call to her mobile phone resulted in the voice mail message. Responsibility lay heavily on his shoulders, and even though his reasoning mind told him not to be such a fool, that she was a grown woman and had her own life to lead, the emotional part of himself, the deep childhood bond between them, surfaced in his mind and threatened by the very nature of things, to defeat the logical side. His flight back to Australia was booked. He would have to leave her soon. If he left without seeing her again, would this be forever on his conscience? He was a troubled man when he returned to the B and B in the early hours of the morning.

Still there was no sign of Mary when he woke and he spent the next day wandering around the streets. He walked down Dundas Street and even went inside *Le Bon*. The gallery was quiet and the statue of Prometheus was gone leaving a space in the room where it had sat for many years. Francesca Fitzwilliam's paintings were off the wall and it looked like another exhibition was about to take place. There was no sign of Martin MacDonald, the gallery manager, and when Oisin enquired as to where he was, he received a curt reply from a rather distracted young woman. It was Mr MacDonald's day off, she said. Mary was not there. He wandered out of the gallery somewhat bemused and decided to search for her at to what had become his favourite coffee lounge off Princes Street.

He sat down at a table at the front of the room so he could watch for people coming in and out. He had planned to take Mary to this coffee lounge before his flight home to Australia. Now it seemed he might never see her again.

****

Oisin woke to hear the noise of the traffic and the monotone sound of a lone pigeon outside his window. He had spent a restless night, tossing and turning in the narrow and uncomfortable bed, and he had dreamed of Mary. In his dream his sister was flying through the air pursued by a pack of seven wolves and she flew, free and fearless, her face a picture of pure joy. This was a younger Mary, the Mary of his childhood, a happier Mary. All the time the wolves snapped at her feet and hands. One of them managed to take hold of her ankle and his jaws locked around it. Mary took no notice but flew on over fields of ripening wheat and rivers that flowed through them. Snow-capped conical mountains appeared out of nowhere. Then the seven wolves turned as one, disappearing from view

264

but Mary glided as graceful as a swan through the air, on towards the mountains, and there astride the highest mountain stood a man dressed in a magician's red and yellow clock. A witch's black hat sat at an odd angle on top of his head and this peculiar hat was adorned with dozens and dozens of shiny red, orange, green and blue precious stones. They sparkled in the light for everything around was dark. Only the magician's face and hat were visible. When Mary saw the magician she flew right through his body. Then Oisin woke up.

It took him a few moments to return to his waking state. Mary was so vivid that he almost felt trapped there with her, flying through the air, pursued by hungry wolves, and all the time feeling the joy that his physical body could appear and disappear as she had in done so in the dream. This small bedroom with its four walls in an Edinburgh Bed and Breakfast establishment was the fantasy. He opened his eyes, yawned and sat on the edge of the bed.

Half an hour later he had washed, shaved and dressed and ready for the day ahead. The aroma of freshly cooked bacon reached his nostrils as he opened the door. He could hear the landlady's voice with her thick Edinburgh accent. She, no doubt, was busy being friendly to the latest paying guests. He could make out the guttural sounds of the Austrians she had told him about. He was in no mood to make conversation with strangers. His plan was to eat, be as civil as he could get away with, and try once again to locate his sister. He was beginning to wonder whether the next course of action would be to approach the police and list Mary as a missing person.

But with all these thoughts fighting for a place in his head, he was far away into another world. He closed the door, turned around, and there in front of him, with hair and face a mess, and her clothes looking the worst for wear, was Mary.

'Oisin, thank God, you're here,' she said. 'What have I done?'

Not waiting for a reply, she started to cry. Tears ran down her cheeks and over a face that looked as if it hadn't been washed for a week.

CHAPTER FOURTEEN

A thousand demons pursued Mary Kelly when she fled from the home of Isabella Luchetta; these demons that taunted and entered into her mind without warning, and left her helpless, powerless, an unwilling victim. Cruel were these demon memories, phantoms that possessed her, and try as she could, she could not defeat them. How she longed to set them packing and be gone for good. How she longed to be free of them. But no, they visited in the night or teased in the morning.

For it was a demon name above all else that haunted Mary Kelly. A few moments before, had Isabella Luchetta not spoken that same terrible name to Oisin, all would have been well. She would have continued sitting, not taking any part in the conversation, as pleasant as it appeared to be, for she had decided earlier that the Luchetta family belonged to Oisin's memory, not hers, but then just as she was drifting off thinking all manner of things, the name of Anton Le Bon was spoken in the room and something within her, an uncontrollable force within, took possession at that dreadful moment. A wild fury it was that came over her, and the name and the painting and all manner of memories, the unresolved pain of ages past, made her lose control of her emotions there and then, and throw the full cup of tea over the painting, and possessed of this demon, the only course of action left was to flee.

The garden at 42 Willow Crescent was vast for a city dwelling and Mary, her mind not in this place, but somewhere else amongst all the demons that had taken over her mind at that particular moment, stood on the stone steps, not knowing what to do next. She had to hide away and cover her head for to stay standing on the steps would mean she had to face those demons, for any minute now Oisin would appear and want to know what had happened. The only thing to do was to escape from these steps for in escaping from there, she would not have to explain about those demons.

Behind a topiary shape resembling an acorn, Mary glimpsed the roof of a building and it was here she ran to, over the carefully trimmed lawn, past the bed of roses to what was a summer house, a wooden framed building painted slate green, a corrugated iron roof with blinds behind the windows, and no one about. She tried the handle of the tinted glass door. It opened into a small, secluded room, a cosy place to hide. There were books and magazines scattered randomly on a glass topped cane coffee table, two cane chairs with comfortable cushions covered with a yellow and red hibiscus flower linen fabric. Various prints of Scottish and Italian scenes added colour to the magnolia painted walls, and there on a shelf at the back of the room above a small sink complete with stainless steel faucets, sat an electric kettle, tea, coffee, and under the shelf, a small fridge. Mary opened the door of the fridge. Inside were two unopened cartons of orange juice, long life milk and some butter and cheese.

This was a place to relax in, to escape to, a hideaway at any time of the year for a small gas heater kept the room warm in the winter and the windows could be opened during the summer months. Mary collapsed onto one of the cane chairs and pulled the tartan rug that she found on another shelf around her shoulders. Outside, it was growing darker. Her body relaxed. She shut her eyes and in a matter of seconds, she fell asleep.

****

'Well, now, what have we here?'

A rough hand shook Mary's shoulder and she woke to see a young man of about twenty years of age with a mass of red hair and freckles on his nose. For one surreal moment, she didn't know where she was. Where was Oisin? He should be here, with her at the Bed and Breakfast for in two days' time he was due to fly back to Australia, and she to return to Ballybeg. They had planned what they would do for their last week together in Edinburgh but here she

269

was, in this small unknown room with a stranger shaking the life out of her.

'Where am I?'

'Well, now, you're in Signorina Isabella's summerhouse. Have you been here all night?'

'I... I can't remember.'

'You're shivering. Best take you over to see Isabella and get something warm into you.'

And the young man took hold of Mary's elbow and helped her to her feet. She felt shaky and was glad she had his arm for support. Her whole body was in some sort of rebellion. All she wanted to do was lie down again but she obediently allowed herself to be helped from the summerhouse. They crossed the lawn to a door at the back of the house which led into the kitchen. The cook with the Zimmer frame was there, preparing breakfast.

'Look what I found in the summerhouse, Aggie,' the young man said to the cook.

The cook turned around and when she saw it was Mary, she frowned. For a second it looked like she was about to threaten Mary and order her to leave but when she saw the look on Mary's face, she softened.

'It's you then,' she said. 'You what threw the tea all over Isabella's painting... took me an hour to clean it up it did. But look at ye...'

'How did she get into the summerhoose?' she

asked the young man as if Mary wasn't there.

'Don't know. Can't get anything out of her,' replied the red head. 'It's over to you now, Aggie,' he said with a wink. 'Got the far garden to weed or Isabella will have my guts for garters!'

He left the kitchen whistling, leaving Mary perching somewhat uncomfortably on one of the kitchen stools.

'Would ye fancy a cup of tea?' asked the cook. Despite outward appearances, she had a kind heart. 'An' dinnae ye be throwin' it round the room naw.'

'Thank you,' replied Mary. Her head hurt.

'I best take ye in to see Isabella,' said the cook when Mary had finished the cup of tea.

Isabella was sitting in the same room as she had been the day before and on the same chair. She was reading a newspaper and when she saw it was Mary with the cook, she shook her head as if in disbelief.

'Well,' she said. 'Have you come back to apologise?'

'I... I don't know. What did I do?'

'You can't remember?'

'Where's Oisin? He was here, wasn't he? I must see him.'

Isabella folded up the newspaper and the cook, who had somehow managed to guide Mary, hold the breakfast tray and walk with her Zimmer, placed the tray with some dexterity, as it held a pot of tea, cup and saucer, a boiled egg and toast, onto a small table next to Isabella.

'That will be all for now, Aggie,' said Isabella.

The cook muttered something under her breath, shuffled away and closed the door behind her. Outside the door, she stopped to listen. This was one conversation that she wanted to hear.

Mary looked around the room. There was no evidence of a broken teacup or stained wallpaper. Francesca Fitzwilliam's painting looked just as it had been; the grey winged horse, nostrils flared, looking very much as if it was escaping, to be free at last from all restraints, and behind the magnificent creature, a kaleidoscope of red, yellow and orange.

'I am too old now to worry about matters that no longer interest me. Nor do I have time or indeed the energy, to judge people's behaviour. But there is just one thing I want to know,' Isabella paused. Her watery brown eyes fixed on Mary's face.

'Why?'

Mary did not answer. The demon had returned and now it had taken up residence once more inside her head. She clenched her fists.

'Something was said here yesterday, wasn't there... something... or someone?' Eighty-five year old Isabella was as astute as ever.

Mary lowered her eyes. The demon with the name was trying its best to take control of her once more, as it had done before and would do again. A struggle began to take place in the mind of Mary as the memory of yesterday's events dawned. The teacup, the painting and the anger all jostled together, and for that ever so brief moment, it looked as if the demon inside her might be gone. But demon thoughts are demon thoughts and the pain of them is real, if not at all understood by others. Mary could not control her demon.

'It was something you said... to Oisin. I'm sorry I broke your teacup.'

'Ah, now I remember. Of course. I remember you too. I was introduced to you

once, years ago... at an art exhibition in London. I almost bought a painting of yours... a seascape.'

Isabella lent forward in her chair to be closer to Mary. Things were becoming clearer to her. She studied the forlorn face of the woman in front of her and into her mind came her own particular demon. What a lot of soul searching had been done and how difficult it was to be released from its clutches. Once she had learned to forgive, it had been easy. The demon banished in an instant, and she was free of it forever. Yes, she wanted this woman to hear what she had to say.

'So you are Mary Kelly, and what a coincidence this is, don't you agree? To think you are Oisin Kelly's sister, the famous Oisin Kelly who my father and Aunt Rosa used to talk about in such glowing terms. But that's years ago, isn't it?' She paused. 'I didn't recognise Oisin yesterday but I have been thinking of him all night. At my age, sleep sometimes doesn't arrive on time as it used to. Never mind.'

Isabella smiled. 'Now, where was I? Oisin... your brother is a brave man... that's what my father said, a brave young man... I remember my cousin, Concetta liked your brother a lot... but then, Concetta sees the best in everyone. I have not been so forgiving.'

Neither woman spoke. The only sound in the room came from the grandfather clock, a Luchetta family heirloom that had sat in the same spot for as long as Isabella could remember. Then Isabella began to eat her breakfast. She had long slender fingers. These same looking fingers she had inherited from the mother she had lost, the mother who had died in childbirth when Isabella was just two years of age. When she finished eating, she wiped her mouth with a paper napkin. Isabella was still as meticulous in her habits as she had always been. Now, at her advanced age, she was never in a hurry.

'I think it was a name that caused you to react in the way you did. Is this not so? Because when I mentioned the name of the art dealer, I saw the anger come into your face, and I am right, aren't I?'

Mary didn't answer. What Isabella had just said was absolutely true. It was mention of the art dealer and hearing his name spoken out aloud to Oisin that had caused the outburst. But she had held the hatred inside her for so long; she wasn't sure whether she wanted to let it go just yet. Hatred is poison but it is also a shield in a peculiar sort of way, and becomes bound like a tight knot inside a person, that to admit to its power can lead to the fear that there is nothing else left to replace it, and emptiness of the soul is a fearful thing to contemplate. This surely was Mary's hatred of Anton Le Bon, the art dealer for he had become so much a part of her very being and been there for so long. To talk about it to a complete stranger was a scary thought indeed. Even having this conversation was enough for Mary to want to flee from the room as she had done so before but she remained pinned to her seat. There was something in Isabella Luchetta's demeanour that demanded she stay.

'I will tell you a story about Anton Le Bon, the famous art dealer and gallery owner. I have... had... a dear friend, Beatrice Caputo. She passed away a few years ago and I miss her still. We were friends all my life, soul mates. To find one true friend in this life is a blessing, Mary Kelly.'

She looked so sad that Mary wondered if she was about to cry and she would never hear anything at all about Anton Le Bon, but Isabella seemed to recover her composure, and a few moments later she continued to talk.

'And it is Beatrice's daughter, Sophia who gave me the painting that so angered you. I do not know why I received such a generous gift, maybe atonement, who knows? Sophia spends money like water. Why, she has bought a huge bronze statue for Alexandro to be shifted back to Italy... I have seen the statue, ugly piece of work, I thought. But I wander... Sophia is married to a count... they have a curious marriage to say the least... but that's another story.'

She paused for a few seconds for her mind was away now with Sophia and Count Alexandro, and the loss of her dear friend, Beatrice, and how short our lives are, her own time here almost gone.

'Beatrice spoke a lot to me about Anton Le Bon. You see, Sophia has always been a problem for her... wilful, spoilt, but she can be so charming at times... maybe that's why I received the painting. But about your art dealer, I first met Anton in Bologna years ago before he became famous. He was with Sophia that day. They were so young and in love. Beatrice and I were enjoying a coffee... such coffees they make... I have not been there for years. This was our favourite place to meet when I was in Bologna but times change... I think Concetta told me that coffee establishment we liked so much on the Piazza Maggiore is no longer there... has been replaced by some American monstrosity... but I digress... please forgive an old woman her ramblings.'

'I was telling you about Anton... Anton was vain then and still is... Beatrice never liked him... but it is a strange thing how men and women attract each other. It's a mystery to me and always has been why Sophia and Anton have never left each other.'

Even to hear the name of Anton Le Bon caused Mary to tighten her hands into fists. She took a few deep breaths. This was difficult for her to keep control. The demon was still there within, mocking her, any minute now it might surface and then she would erupt, run out of the room, and away from this old woman with her memories.

'Anton Le Bon has a reputation for liking young girls. Sophia knows this but she stays with him. I have often wondered that the reason could be to spite her mother and nothing at all to do with Anton, but I am a cynic in these matters. Maybe Sophia does love him. Stranger things happen. Beatrice thought Anton a monster. I do not like him but I have only met him a few times. When I was younger, I sometimes visited his gallery in Dundas Street but I rarely saw him there, and even when I did, he was rather cool towards me. Maybe because I knew too much about him... or could it be that I have never bought a painting from him?' Isabella laughed.

'He is famous in the art world and young girls are attracted to him for all manner of reasons. And I think you were, along with all the other innocent girls, a victim to his excesses, and that is why you hate him even now?'

Mary heard the words and an image as clear in her mind as if it was yesterday, this image appeared before her, an image of a man, and an art gallery, and a young girl full of hope.

'I was just sixteen,' she whispered.

Isabella, her hearing gone observed Mary's lips moving but in that moment of awareness that exists sometimes between two women, understood what was being whispered for hadn't she, too, suffered at the hands of men?

Mary sat in silence in this room of many memories but in her mind she was no longer there. She was a young girl again outside an art gallery, newly opened in Dublin, a portfolio under her arm, and meeting a man who promised her the world. Mary Kelly, the rebel from Ballybeg as innocent as a new born, and the shame that came after.

The antique grandfather clock struck eleven o'clock. Time, measured in seconds, passed by, and then came the fleeting images, ephemeral ones in the minds of these two women for neither were young girls full of expectation but women of a certain age, remembering.

'I had better go,' Mary said, louder this time so that Isabella could hear this time.

She stood up, unsure of what to do next or whether she should leave or not. Then she did something unexpected and she didn't know why. Something good done on an impulse can mean a lot to another, and this was one of those occasions. She shook the withered hand of Isabella Luchetta with its brown spots of age, and gave it a gentle squeeze. Then she softly kissed the old lady on the cheek.

'I have to go.'

'It's over, Mary Kelly,' Isabella murmured.

'It's not over... not yet,' was Mary's answer.

****

Mary heard her phone ring as she walked the streets of Edinburgh. It was Oisin. He had been ringing all morning but she didn't answer. Her mind was everywhere; everything around her did not seem real, being in Edinburgh, walking along these unfamiliar streets felt like a dream. And one day she would wake up and it would all be over.

When she returned to the Bed and Breakfast it

was late in the evening and no light shone under Oisin's door. She turned the key in her own room and sank onto the bed, her body crying out for sleep, her mind longing for peace. For an hour she lay there, staring at the ceiling and the cream fabric lightshade above her head, and then she closed her eyes.

CHAPTER FIFTEEN

Kilgoolga was dust and distance. There hadn't been a drop of rain for six months. Under the pitiless blue sky Oisin Kelly struggled to adapt to his surroundings for his restless spirit could find no peace. Things had changed in three months. He had changed.

Somehow, and he didn't know why, his mind stayed in Edinburgh, and he thought at times he even left it in Ballybeg. Though his body had moved to the other side of the earth away from the huddled villages, green fields and soft light to the emptiness of Kilgoolga, where a bright unforgiving sun and parched earth greeted him every morning, he couldn't escape these feelings. Everything in Kilgoolga seemed distant, even Claire was different, and he had so loved his wife. He began to wonder if they, too, had drifted away into the distance.

The return was amicable enough between them, and he was glad to see her again but to speak about what he experienced in the three months they had been apart from each other, was nigh on impossible. That distance thing again, he decided. And he did think of Mary a lot as well as Edinburgh and Ballybeg. How could he explain his sister to Claire? How could he explain anything?

Mary had refused to go to the airport to say

goodbye to him. Instead, he spent his last day in Edinburgh doing all those things that are done before a long journey. The B and B owner had been sorry to see him go. She told him that if he was ever back in Edinburgh, he was more than welcome to stay with her again, at a reduced rate, which rather surprised Oisin given her earlier aloofness.

Then Mary announced that she was leaving as well but she wouldn't be drawn as to where she was going. Oisin wondered if she intended to return to Ballybeg but when he suggested that, she just shrugged her shoulders. He felt responsible somehow. Filial feelings run deep; he had seen the very best of Mary, and experienced the very worst in their time together. It was best to remember her as she was rather than dwell on the other, darker side of her character. That way he reasoned he could cope with the darker side.

Their parting had been a strained affair. They shook hands like strangers, and it was only when he wheeled his travelling bag to the door of the B and B, and picked up his overcoat, that she showed any emotion. She became a different Mary all of a sudden; her arms around his body and tears in her eyes.

'I'll never see you again, Oisin.'

'What do ye mean? Of course, we'll see each other again. We've still got a few good years left in us... ?'

'I'll *never* see you again,' she repeated the words.

These were the words that stayed with him. They pierced his head like tiny daggers, and try as he could, he couldn't rid himself of them. He tried to adjust to his life in Kilgoolga and with Claire, and be content but it was a hopeless situation. Mary's face was forever before him.

A few days later he unpacked the Francesca Fitzwilliam painting of the winged horse that he had bought for his daughter, Suze on an impulse. Had he known that the sight of a similar Fitzwilliam painting hanging on the wall in Isabella Luchetta's front room would have caused such a violent reaction from his sister, he would have quite happily left his one in the gallery, but hindsight is all well and good. The purchase had been made in good faith, and anyhow he rather liked the painting.

He was disappointed that Suze had disappeared in her campervan, destination unknown, and hadn't been heard of for weeks. But then, he and Suze had a troubled relationship most of the time. He thought the gift of the painting might have helped heal some of the wounds between them. So he showed the painting to Claire who wasn't impressed.

'I don't like it,' she said. Claire could always be

relied upon for her directness. This was one of her characteristics that had appealed to him when they first met. She called a spade a spade.

'What don't ye like about it?'

'I can't understand it. The horse is well done, I suppose... but I can't get my head around all those blues and greens splashed around behind it. What on earth made you buy it?'

'I rather liked it and I thought that Suze might as well.'

'Doubt it. Think you wasted your money this time,' replied Claire and that was the end of the matter.

Oisin would not be intimidated. He hung the painting up in the small room at the back of the house where he liked to escape to when things got out of hand. Here, in the quiet room, he could study the painting. For some reason, there was comfort there for him amongst all the imagery and the colour. He wasn't at all bothered about his wife's reaction. At other times he thought about Anton Le Bon, the gallery in Dundas Street, and often he wondered why his sister had hated the man so much. He decided one day that she might have known Anton Le Bon in an intimate way, and when he thought of that, he felt annoyed. He decided that it would have been helpful if Mary had confided in him. There had been opportunities to speak about it in Edinburgh but maybe it was too difficult for her to talk to a brother she hadn't seen for years. The two of them weren't exactly strangers, but then they weren't exactly friends either.

Was it too much beyond the bounds of possibility that if there had been a relationship between Anton and Mary, and it had been an ugly one, the result might have been that Mary lost control of her mind?

****

One evening, Oisin joined his wife to watch the news on the television, to sit beside her in the familiar room, and try to regain some of the closeness they used to enjoy before he went away. He wanted to think that nothing had changed between them but in his heart, he knew that was not so. They would live out their lives together as familiar strangers and at the end of it all, if it was he or Claire who passed away first, the other would grieve for a while but life would go on.

Oisin settled himself into his comfortable old chair and turned on the television. There were wars in foreign places followed by a report about a murder in a remote part of South Australia, and then on the screen in front of a surprised Oisin came the report of a death of an art dealer and galley owner, famous the world over. And there was a picture of Anton Le Bon, looking just like the fleeting image that Oisin had seen of him in Edinburgh.

'I know this man,' he almost shouted. 'I bought the painting you didn't like from his gallery in Edinburgh!'

'What are you talking about?'

'This man, Anton Le Bon.'

'Well, looks like he's been murdered,' said Claire. 'Stabbed to death... mustn't have been much of a man if that happened to him. Now I know why I didn't like the painting!'

Oisin didn't reply. He listened in a kind of daze as the report went on to say that Anton Le Bon had been found in an alleyway in Edinburgh with multiple stab wounds. Although he was rushed to the Edinburgh Infirmary, he died a few hours later from the wounds. Police have not been able to establish a motive for the killing nor have they been able to track done the perpetrator. If anyone was in the area at the time and seen anything suspicious they are encouraged to come forward. A tearful young artist, Francesca Fitzwilliam was interviewed next. She spoke in glowing terms about how the gallery owner had been such an influence on herself, and other young artists. The report concluded with a tribute to Anton and mention of his great contribution to the art world.

A few moments later, an image of a triumphant Australian cricket team appeared on the screen. They had recaptured the Ashes from the English and would be bringing the trophy home to a warm welcome. Oisin turned off the television.

****

Oisin drove into the township of Kilgoolga in a hope that he might recapture some of the feelings for the place. For the first few years of living in the remote township, he had felt alien, almost an intruder in another world, but as he adjusted to his new surroundings, and after he met Claire, things changed for him. His life became routine, and if at times, a banal existence, he had grown content in this environment on the other side of the earth. All had changed now after three months away. He reasoned that he should be glad to be back for this was the place where destiny had led him but try as he could, he could not settle, and then guilt visited him which made matters worse.

He parked the car under the bottle tree in the main street and sat there, remembering. There were a few people about and a brown dog of uncertain parentage curled up outside the butcher's shop. People seemed to know the dog for one or two spoke to him, and a woman with a shopping bag offered him a treat. The dog accepted the offering and wagged its tail in thanks.

Oisin got out of the car and stretched. Age was catching up with him and his joints ached. It took him a few seconds to persuade his legs to move after sitting for a while. The main street hadn't changed in the three months he had been away. The shops were the same. A thin layer of red dust covered the footpath. Footprints were visible everywhere. Some shopkeepers swept the footpath outside their shop but it was a thankless task. No sooner had they got rid of the dust before another gust of wind brought more. When the rains came this same footpath would be transformed into red watery mud, and there would be something different for the people to complain about.

For this Irishman, the walk along the main street of Kilgoolga was a trip into nostalgia. Past the Commercial Hotel where the enigmatic Eleanor Bradshaw had seduced his soul, to the War Memorial to remember when he had sat, newly arrived in Kilgoolga, and studied the names of the fallen. It was there that he had flirted with Claire as she tottered along on high heels from the High School, struggling with her heavy bag. Perhaps that was the day that he knew Claire would become his wife, if he played his cards right. They were happier days.

In this street of memories there was Hope MacFarlane, the nurse who married his broken Vietnam veteran brother-in-law, Harry, the same nurse whose body he had desired, and no one but the two of them ever knew of this slight transgression, least of all Claire.

He walked back to the car slowly, deep in thought, still there in a different time, knowing deep down that the past had to be put to rest, finally and for good, and all this nostalgia was just an excuse for not wanting to get on with the present. It was then that his phone rang, interrupting his thoughts and bringing him with a jolt into reality. It was Ryan ringing from Ballybeg.

'Is that you, Oisin?' Ryan's voice sounded far away but then it was. That miracle of the twentieth century, the mobile phone, defied distance and Ryan could have been speaking from next door.

'Aye. What time is it over there?'

Funny how these calls from the other side of the earth always seem to focus on time. It was as if it brought things closer somehow.

'Eight o'clock at night... but Oisin I'm ringing to tell ye, something's happened... it's Mary...'

'Mary?'

'Aye. Bad news, I'm afraid.'

'What's she done now?'

'Oisin... Uncle Oisin... ' There was a pause.

'She's dead.'

'Dead?'

'Aye. Drowned.'

'What do ye mean... drowned?'

'Aye. She went into the Forth at Queensferry. Her body washed up on the shore. No suspicious circumstances. Death by misadventure the verdict is, so they say... ?'

Ryan's voice sounded far away all of a sudden.

'We're bringing the body back to Ballybeg... seems only right. She wouldn't want to be in Scotland... even though she hated Ballybeg, like she was forever tellin' us, her spirit is here an' that's where she would want to be.'

'We've a space for her... in the Kelly plot... next to her mother,' he added. It looked like Ryan had taken charge of the whole procedure. Where were Frankie and Declan?

'When's the funeral?' Oisin asked then, rather lamely, best to focus on reality at a time like this.

'Next Tuesday,' came the reply. Things had to be done.

There was a brief silence and then Ryan spoke,

'I don't think she would want ye to come back for the funeral though, Oisin.'

'No.'

He had said goodbye to his sister in Edinburgh,

those three weeks.

'One last thing, Oisin,' Ryan's voice became more businesslike. 'There's a letter here for you from Mary. She mustn't have known your address out there and wanted me to forward it to ye. We don't get many letters these days, do we? Mary wasn't one for emails. I'll get it in the post in the next day or two.'

****

Claire was busy in the kitchen making vegetable soup. When she saw her husband's face, she knew that something had happened.

'What's wrong, love?' she asked.

'It's my sister, Mary,' he said. 'She's dead.'

'Oh, Oisin... I'm sorry...'

'Aye. Drowned. They say it was an accident... but, Claire,' he looked into her eyes and she saw the sadness there, as only a woman could, 'my sister was a troubled soul...?'

He wanted someone to hold him; to put their arms around him, and tell him it would be alright, as a mother to a child. He wanted desperately to know he was loved.

Claire did just that. She wrapped her arms around his chest and said nothing. There were tears in Oisin's eyes. Nothing mattered now to him but the present, and it was a precious moment indeed, for here in his wife's arms Oisin Kelly, the exiled Irishman was home.

EPILOGUE

Under the coolibah tree where he had spent many a long contemplative hour, was where Oisin decided he wanted to read the letter from Mary. It was a brief note, the handwriting written in her usual flamboyant style. It looked like the words had been put on the paper in a hurry.

He read the letter twice.

Old sins cast long shadows.

Then he folded the letter. With care, he returned it to the envelope. He would never read the words again.

Oisin's story continues as told by his daughter, Suze...

****

CHAPTER ONE

My father had the soul of a poet. His name was Oisin Kelly and he came from Ireland. As far as I know he never wrote a line of poetry in his whole life but then, there were many layers in my father's life, and I knew very little about any of them.

My own life has many unspoken layers as well, and if my father had known them, he would have been as surprised as I was when I uncovered his secret layers. We were estranged for many years and it was only after his death that I discovered something about this very ordinary man who lived an extraordinary life.

For all these reasons, I have decided to tell his story, my way.

ACKNOWLEDGEMENTS

All writers need editors and readers.

I am indebted to Oliver Eade for his editorial expertise and the cover design. This book would not have seen the light of day without his help. Thank you, Oliver.

To fellow writer Maura Kennedy Fair, many thanks for taking the time to read the book before publication.

I would also like to thank Wendy Leighton Porter at Silver Quill Publishing for continuing to support my writing.

ABOUT THE AUTHOR

Iona Carroll is the author of the Oisin Kelly novels. Her literary career started as a librarian and teacher. She has led creative writing workshops with the emphasis on short story writing. An Australian, she now lives in the Scottish Borders with her husband and her wirehaired dachshund, Millie.

ABOUT SILVER QUILL

Silver Quill Publishing

Silver Quill Publishing is an established publishing group producing fabulous books for children, teens, young – and not so young – adults. Take a look at our website, meet our authors and browse through the titles we have to offer.
Every book is a thrill with Silver Quill.

www.silverquillpublishing.com